"Itching for adventure as the war reach[...] twenty-year-old Clara Wilson runs away [...] After arriving in battle-torn France, patchin[...] soon regrets her impulsive decision. But as [...] turned-soldier, she makes a promise that v[...] dramatically than war. Emily T. Wierenga's *A Promise in Pieces* is not to be missed—a poignant, beautifully crafted story that will leave you wanting more from this talented debut novelist."
—Suzanne Woods Fisher, award-winning, best-selling author of the Stoney Ridge Seasons series

"Wierenga is a stunning new writer. I became so engrossed in this riveting story, I grieved to see it end."
—Serena B. Miller, award-winning author of *The Measure of Katie Calloway* and *A Promise to Love*

"Beautifully rendered with depth and compassion, *A Promise in Pieces* is a celebration of joy in a special quilt that commemorates the miracle of new life and offers healing to the brokenhearted. With a bright new voice in Christian fiction, Emily Wierenga's debut novel is one to be cherished. Tender and heartfelt from the first page to the last and a worthy addition to the Quilts of Love series."
—Carla Stewart, award-winning author of *Chasing Lilacs* and *Sweet Dreams*

"Emily T Wierenga's debut novel, *A Promise in Pieces*, grabbed hold of my heart and didn't let go until I read the end, and even then, the characters have lingered in my mind. Well-written, this touching story will leave you wanting more from this talented new author. Novel Rocket and I give it our highest recommendation. It's a 5-star *must* read."
—Ane Mulligan, president of NovelRocket, author of *Chapel Springs Revival*

"Let your heart be inspired by this beautiful new voice in Christian fiction!"
—Anita Higman, author of *A Marriage in Middlebury*

"*A Promise in Pieces* is an endearing story of love and sacrifice, masterfully told by Emily Wierenga. This lovely book, part of the Quilts of Love series, is itself like a quilt. It is stitched together with lyrical prose and likable characters, and readers will find themselves wanting to wrap themselves in the warmth of the story."
—Jennifer Dukes Lee, author of *Love Idol: Letting Go of Your Need for Approval—and Seeing Yourself Through God's Eyes*

"Drawing readers into a beautifully woven tale, Wierenga seamlessly stitches together the stories of rich characters in this inspiring tale of family and faith, love and war. You won't want to put it down at night!"
—Margot Starbuck, author of *The Girl in the Orange Dress*

"Both heart wrenching and heartwarming, *A Promise in Pieces* is a wonderful read that reveals just how lives torn apart can be stitched back together again—beautifully and with a fair portion of grace. Compellingly told in a voice that is both direct and lyrical, seamlessly woven so that the world of today reverberates with the reality of the past, this book will leave you reflecting on the importance of family, believing that chance encounters can yield friendships to last a lifetime, and yearning for another novel from Emily Wierenga."
—Karen Schreck, author of *Sing for Me* and *While He Was Away*

"*A Promise in Pieces* is stunningly written. I couldn't put this captivating book down!"
—Kate Lloyd, author of CBA best-selling novels *Leaving Lancaster* and *Pennsylvania Patchwork*

"This sweet story reminds us of the power of a promise and, more importantly, the unfailing love of our God . . . who keeps every promise ever made to us. Emily's voice is a lovely match for this beautiful novel."
—Deidra Riggs, founder of JumpingTandem, managing editor of *The High Calling*

"Like a beautifully embroidered patchwork quilt, *A Promise in Pieces* expertly weaves the universal themes of love, loyalty, grief, family, and friendship into a richly compelling and moving story. Penned with the gentle lyricism and breathtaking poignancy typical of Wierenga's writing, this page-turning story will breathe hope and light into your heart from the first page to the last."
—Michelle DeRusha, author of *Spiritual Misfit*

A Promise in Pieces

Quilts of Love Series

Emily T. Wierenga

a novel approach to faith

A Promise in Pieces

Copyright © 2014 by Emily T. Wierenga

ISBN-13: 978-1-4267-5885-0

Published by Abingdon Press, P.O. Box 801, Nashville, TN 37202

www.abingdonpress.com

Published in association with the MacGregor Literary Agency

Library of Congress Cataloging-in-Publication Data

Wierenga, Emily T., 1980-
 A Promise in Pieces / Emily T. Wierenga.
    pages cm. — (Quilts of Love Series)
 ISBN 978-1-4267-5885-0 (binding: soft back, adhesive perfect binding, pbk. : alk. paper) 1.
Quilts—Fiction. 2. Nurses—Fiction. 3. Quiltmakers—Fiction. 4. Christian fiction. I. Title.
 PS3623.I3848P76 2014
 813'.6—dc23

                                                                        2013041837

Printed in the United States of America

1 2 3 4 5 6 7 8 9 10 / 19 18 17 16 15 14

Other books in the Quilts of Love Series

Dedicated to my grandmother, Winifred Dow,
who lost her friend and brother, Bill,
to the Second World War.

Acknowledgments

To my agent, Sandra Bishop, for being ever there and ever believing, thank you. You are a gift.

To Amanda Batty, who helped me find words—you are a true friend.

To my grandparents, Norman and Winifred Dow, who provided inspiration for this story—I love you.

To my husband and sons for giving me up while I wrote and edited—you are my life.

To my editors, Ramona Richards, Teri Wilhelms, and Susan Cornell—thank you for honing my words.

To my marketing manager, Cat Hoort—you sent my words soaring.

And to my Lord and Savior Jesus Christ, the Word, without whom I would have no voice—thank you for being my friend.

PART 1

WAR

Nothing except a battle lost can be half so melancholy as a battle won.

—Arthur Wellesley, First Duke of Wellington, 1815

1

2000

Noah looked like his father, and she hadn't noticed it before. But here in the backseat of a Dodge Caravan, strewn with skateboarding magazines and CDs, there was time enough to see it in the young man whose long legs stretched from the seat beside her. To see the freckles dusting her grandson's cheeks, the way his hair poked up like a hayfield, and how his eyes grabbed at everything.

Up front, Oliver asked Shane to adjust the radio, the static reminding Clara of the white noise she used to make with a vacuum or a fan to calm her newborns. The first one being Shane, her eldest, the one in the passenger seat turning now to laugh at his father, who wrinkled his long nose as Shane tried to find a classical station.

Then, Vivaldi's *Four Seasons*, and Clara could see Oliver smiling, pleased, and she remembered the way he'd looked over at her in church so long ago with the same expression: as though he'd finally found what he'd been looking for.

Noah was playing a game on one of those Nintendo machines. He noticed her watching him and said, "Do you want to give it a try, Grandma?" He looked so eager.

Gone were the days of Hardy Boys and marbles. "Sure!" Clara said, mustering enthusiasm as she took the tiny gadget. Then she saw what he was playing. Some kind of shooting game with uniformed men and guns and she nearly dropped it.

"I'm sorry, it's too complicated for an old woman like me," she said, handing it back and turning to stare out the window, at Maryland passing by, wondering what a kid in high school could know about war.

They were taking the George Washington Memorial Parkway, one of Clara's favorite drives, which would carry them from her home state to Mount Vernon, Virginia. They were passing through Glen Echo, north of Washington, DC. And Clara remembered the story her daddy had told her, on one of their summer holidays, about her namesake, Clara Barton, who'd spent the last fifteen years of her life here. The founder of the American Red Cross, Ms. Barton had tirelessly provided aid to wounded troops during the Civil War. She had dedicated her life to serving those in need, Daddy said.

On that holiday, Clara—only eight years old at the time— had decided she would do the same. After all, she had been named after Ms. Barton.

"Something wrong, Grandma?" Noah said.

Shane turned in the front seat. His green eyes met hers, and it seemed only yesterday she had brought him home wrapped in the quilt—the one cleaned, pressed, and folded, lying in the back of their van.

Shane's eyebrows rose and Clara shrugged, feeling cold in her white cardigan even though it was late June. It had been more than fifty years.

"Fifty years," she said, more to herself than anything, and the van was quiet. She'd had these moments before, many of them. Moments landing her in the past, amongst broken and dead bodies, for there hadn't been enough beds in Normandy.

Oliver peered at her now in the rearview, through his glasses, and she should give his hair a trim, she thought. It sprouted silver around his ears, and when had her soldier-husband aged? At what point between them marrying and adopting Shane and giving birth to two others had his hair turned gray?

Noah was tucking the game away now, saying, "I don't need to play this right now. What are you thinking about, Grandma?"

And she wiped at her eyes, moist, and cleared her throat and told herself to smarten up.

It was sixteen and a half hours to New Orleans, where they were heading for a family vacation, and she should make the most of the time she had with this boy who knew nothing of the miracle of the quilt in the back. Who knew nothing of loss, and this was good. But there is a need for history to plant itself in the hearts of its children.

"Do you know about Clara Barton?" she said. Noah shook his head.

"She was a woman of great character. The founder of the American Red Cross. This whole area is a National Historic Site in her name, and she didn't want it. All she wanted was to help people. In 1891, two men, Edwin and Edward Baltzley, offered Clara land for a house in an effort to draw people to this area. They offered her land, as well as free labor for building the house, believing people would come in flocks to see the home of the woman who founded the Red Cross.

"Clara was clever. As all women of the same name are," and here, she winked at Noah who laughed. "She had been looking for a new place to serve as headquarters for the Red Cross, so she took them up on it. She used the home originally as a warehouse for disaster-relief supplies, then reworked it and moved in six years later.

"A newly built electric trolley that ran into Washington brought in crowds of people to a nearby amusement park. When a new manager took over the park in 1906, he offered to buy Clara's home and turn it into a hotel. She refused, so he then tried to drive her out. Apparently, he built a slow-moving scenic railway right by her house, with a station by her front door. When it failed to work, he erected a Ferris wheel in front of her house. Can you imagine? It is said Clara loved the lights from the wheel. She served as president of the Red Cross until 1904 and kept living in the house until her death, eight years later, at age ninety. She said the moon used to always shine at Glen Echo."

Noah's eyes were fixed on her. "What a woman," he said.

Clara nodded. "I know. She's the reason I became a nurse. And went off to war when Daddy told me not to."

It was quiet in the car and then Shane said, "You can't stop there, Mom! Tell him the story!"

Oliver's eyes shining in the mirror, Vivaldi on the radio, and Maryland's fields of corn and hay waving graceful good-byes.

"You sure?" she said to Noah.

He folded his hands in his lap. "I'm all yours, Grandma."

And so, she began.

2

1943

It was the first day of summer. I was twenty-one years old, single, and just graduated nursing school—Eva, too. She was my best friend, ever since grade school. Oh, how her long hair flew like yellow birds as we skipped down Main Street in our little town of Smithers. She was always the pretty one, and I was the smart one, but at the time we were just two girls celebrating.

And then we saw the United Service Organization Club, or the USO.

War was happening on the radio and in our pantries. We all had ration stamps by then and Mama kept saving tin because "we all have to do our part," she told us, in the faded pink apron she always wore.

Daddy kept preaching the same sermon to a congregation of about ten or fifteen women, babies on their knees, and the elderly all huddled together, muttering prayers. He talked to them of peace and turning the other cheek, but no one was listening anymore. Peace just seemed like a cruel kind of joke, and everyone just wanted their men home.

It made me kind of mad the way Daddy would stand there in his preacher's collar at the pulpit in Smithers First Christian Church, singing "Peace Like a River," when all of those babies had no daddies. But I was pretty young so I just slipped out the back as soon as the sermon was done, and Eva and I, we'd go swimming in the river and forget the whole thing. Until we went home and all we had for supper was horse meat or fried Spam because we'd run out of rations since Mama was always giving ours away. Like we weren't suffering, too.

Anyway, Eva was like my sister because I was an only child and she lived a couple of blocks from us, in a fancy house with white siding and pillars. Her daddy was the mayor.

We lived above the Main Street Diner, which closed down when people stopped having money to do anything. Pretty much all of Main Street had shut down in Smithers, and all we had was the USO, which opened up after Pearl Harbor happened.

I'll always remember taking the bus home from my first semester at Johns Hopkins two-year nursing program, December 7, 1941, the world all white and celestial outside, and seeing Mama staring out the window with an empty mug in her hand and Daddy behind her, his hand on her shoulder, and hearing President Roosevelt on the kitchen radio saying the Japanese had bombed Pearl Harbor. "This is no joke," he said over the airwaves. "This is war."

The United States and Britain attacked Japan, and four days later, Hitler declared war on the United States, and Mama rocked a lot in her wooden chair while Daddy preached about peace, and I studied hard at nursing school to become like Clara Barton.

The USO was the first in Maryland they said, and for a while it was one of those places you just kind of look at like it's a candy store and you're a hungry kid. It was all bright and sparkly, full of men in uniform with pretty girls on their arms. Eva and I would climb a tree across from the club and pretend we were those ladies with their curled hair and their laughs.

But then the soldiers shipped out and the place became like an empty bottle of wine, attracting flies and smelling slightly sour. From time to time a woman would emerge, looking tired as all women did those days, and sometimes there were newly drafted boys with shine still on their shoes. But the building mostly sat waiting. As we all did.

Eva and I had never actually seen inside, so the day we were skipping up and down Main Street, celebrating our freedom, we decided to try it. We decided to put on lipstick and nice dresses and wait for servicemen to treat us to a night on the town. So we pulled out our fanciest, least-faded prints and ironed them because it had been years since we'd had any material to sew from, and we took cranberries and crushed them and tried to make our lips red but then we just sneaked into Eva's mom's bedroom and used her lipstick, because she was a fine lady. She always wore pearls and smelled like lilacs. Mama smelled like flour and lotion.

We fluffed our hair and smoothed our dresses and walked with our heads held high all the way down Main Street to the USO.

The woman inside who greeted us hardly looked at us, just kind of nodded wearily to the back of the room where there was a bar and a Ping-Pong table and some old men staring at their drinks. The air was kind of fuzzy, and the jukebox played Bing Crosby like it was trying too hard.

We hadn't known it would be so easy, and our heads weren't near so high as we stepped in our mamas' high heels to the back of the room and sat on stools and ordered Shirley Temples.

"Let's get out of here," Eva said in a whisper, her blonde hair hiding her face from the bartender who seemed just shy of death. I was about to respond when the old man at the other end of the bar asked us if we'd seen his son.

"He looks like his mother, God rest her soul," the guy said, and I still remember him like it was yesterday. He had the longest white beard, his eyes were gray puddles, and his fingers trembled around a glass of what must have been Scotch, although I wouldn't have known it then. All I knew was Daddy's communion wine, which was actually Concord grape juice.

"They drafted him two years ago, and he used to send these letters," he said in a voice so muffled we had to sit very still. "He'd tell me all about the war like it was all exciting and mysterious, but then the letters stopped coming."

His fingers trembled, his wet eyes hid behind his lids, and he swallowed, his beard moving up and down. We looked down at our Shirley Temples.

Here we were, all dressed up and playing games when real people were dying.

So we moved closer to this man who said his name was Roger, and we asked him more about his son, and his eyes just kind of popped open. And he told us stories. He told how his son, Sam, used to pick flowers for everyone he met, and he said, "I would always make fun of him, like he wasn't supposed to do that because he was a boy," said Roger, "but now I'd let him pick as many flowers as he wanted to. I'd say go and pick as many flowers as you want to, but I can't," and we patted his shaky hands and nodded because it was all we could do.

But later, when we left, the sky turning all purple and red the way it does before the sun goes down—like the skin of heaven is bruising or something—we didn't even say good night to each other. We just went each to our own homes, and I scrubbed off my lipstick and took off my dress and wore my oldest, scratchiest pajamas to bed and prayed for forgiveness all night and into dawn.

I barely slept that night. Come morning, a pebble struck my window, and I opened it. Eva stood there. "Come on, we need to go," she said.

"Where?" I asked, and she said down to the Red Cross recruiting center to sign up with the Army Nurse Corps.

So I shimmied out of my window and down the old oak tree the way I'd always done, and we went off to the military recruiting office to enlist.

———

It was a bit humiliating, stripping down so they could make sure we were fit for the army and I stared at a nail in the wall and Eva looked the other way and later we admitted we were both thinking about the tree branch in Eva's backyard where we sat every sunny afternoon when we were young, reading comics and braiding each other's hair and laughing about boys. Because the tree was our safe place.

Then the doctor did my physical exam and found a heart murmur and said normally they wouldn't let someone in this condition go, but they were desperate. So he took the sheet of paper stating I had a heart murmur and tore it in two, right in front of me, and signed another one saying I was fine.

My good conservative upbringing told me it was wrong, but I was ready for wrong. I'd been good and right my whole life, and all it had amounted to was a Bible by my bed and a picture of Jesus as a shepherd on my wall, while other girls my age had posters of Jimmy Stewart. And Jimmy had put his career on hold to enlist, so I decided I would, too, as I signed the forms saying I now belonged to the Army Nurse Corps. "Free a man to fight," the posters said. The roles were all scattered and reversed, and women were raising families and fixing machinery and delivering mail and driving trucks and forecasting weather, and no one was sleeping. The whole country was just kind of stumbling around in a mad state of insomnia. Roosevelt was on the radio, saying, "I regret to tell you that many American lives have been lost," and it was enough to keep us awake and fighting in our own humble ways. Even if it meant just fighting at home so the men could go abroad, but Eva and I would join the ranks of women who'd already signed up to care for the wounded, the ranks led so many years ago by Clara Barton.

A nurse had to be between twenty-one and forty years old. We entered the corps as officers, usually as second lieutenants, but our rank was not equal to that of men. We weren't that advanced. It wouldn't be until after the war that we'd earn the same privileges as the men. Nevertheless, there were more than twelve thousand nurses in the corps, and we weren't told where we were going. We were just shipped off blindly, like we were cattle; some were sent to Alaska, others to Australia, still others to North Africa and Europe, and some to places we'd never even heard of.

Our parents didn't know. We would be leaving on the train for military training in Virginia in one week, and it was such a long week. Mama kept looking at me strangely, and Daddy was even quieter than usual. Then one night over canned beans and dry toast, because we had no butter, I couldn't stand the silence anymore.

"Eva and I are thinking of signing up with the army," I kind of blurted out, and Daddy pushed back his plate and his chair and crossed his arms and breathed deeply, like he was in labor. Mama just sat holding a spoon midway to her mouth while the clock ticked brashly.

I wanted to break the clock.

Daddy pulled out a red-and-white handkerchief and wiped his forehead and Mama set her spoon down and I braced myself. I was small for my age, but I had a big temper, and they knew this. The floor was thick with eggshells.

"Clara Anne," Daddy said, and I shuddered at the sound of my full name. "Why would you go and do that? You know where this family stands on the issue of war," and Mama hung her head because she still collected tin cans and saved cooking grease and took lunch down to the women who worked long hours in the factories.

"You know we believe what Jesus said about turning the other cheek. How do you plan to save souls while you're killing them?"

I began to shake but clenched my teeth and tried to pray because I didn't want to blow up. I knew it wouldn't help. It never had. "Daddy, I'm not going to be killing anybody. I am going to help the soldiers who are wounded."

Daddy shook his head and wiped at the corner of his mouth with a napkin. "In my opinion, if you're helping the soldiers who are killing people, then you're basically killing people."

Mama pushed back her chair and stood, filled up the kettle, and began piling dishes in the sink. "Anyone want a cup of tea?" she asked, her back to us, shoulders hunched, and I knew she was trying not to say anything. Mama and Daddy hadn't agreed on things in years, but she never spoke poorly of him. Instead, she made tea.

"Really, Marie, at a time like this?" Daddy was standing now and beginning to pace. I realized suppertime was over and began to excuse myself when he told me point-blank I wasn't going anywhere.

Mama and I both sat down in our chairs, and Daddy took on his preaching voice. "The people in this town are looking to me for guidance. What will they think when my own daughter goes off to serve in a war I don't believe in? If I don't have any control over my own household, how can I run a church?"

I bristled. Mama looked down at her lap, and the clock ticked.

Then I looked at Daddy's steamed-up face, like a Christmas ham, and his eyes all tiny and narrow, and I knew this was a lost cause. I knew he wouldn't let it go until I did because we were both stubborn that way, so I just nodded and said I understood, I wouldn't sign up, and I was sorry for upsetting him, and could I please have some tea now, Mama?

Daddy adjusted his belt and blew his nose on his handkerchief. He sat down in his chair and smiled to himself and said, "Yes, a cup of tea sounds lovely, Marie. Thank you."

And Mama obediently rose.

That night, as Daddy snored and the wind blew at my gingham curtains, another pebble flew against my window, and I climbed out of the house with my bag.

At the bottom of the diner I whispered good-bye, in my mind, to Mama, and "Sorry, Mama, and I'll miss you, Mama."

Then Eva and I stepped into the darkness, toward the station.

3

July 1943

We knew we were supposed to feel somber or something because this was war, but we were too young and the gunshots too far away, so we laughed a lot on the train ride as night sped by in a blur of trees and sky and fields.

We had each raided our pantries before we left, and all I'd found were some stale peanuts and a small package of sugar I knew Mama was saving for someone who needed it, but I figured I was that person. So we licked our fingers and tasted the sugar the whole four hours to Camp Lee, Virginia, and by the time we got there, we were so giddy we were stumbling around like it had been gin.

When the conductor called our stop we smoothed our hair and our dresses and gathered our bags and stepped out onto a platform as morning lit up the world. The sun looked like a fireball, striking the trees and bushes, and I thought of the story of Moses and the burning bush and wondered if God was trying to speak to me.

And for a moment I felt guilty, thinking about God and picturing Daddy snoring on his pillow and Mama bringing me toast and tea in bed and finding me gone. She'd be shaking

Daddy awake, and he'd be shoving on his glasses and pacing the room and calling the police and preaching at the walls, but, no, I couldn't think this way. I might cave if I did.

I shook my head and forced myself to step out of the train station into the morning light and the more I walked, the less concerned I became with Eva beside me and blue sky above us and hayfields spinning gold all around.

Our bags were threadbare and our shoes worn, but we were two girls on a mission and nothing could stop us. Nothing, except getting lost, and eventually we had to stop because we were. Desperately lost.

We turned around and all we saw were fields. At the train station it had said, "Camp Lee, 30 miles," but it's a lot of miles for two girls running on a single packet of sugar and no sleep, so we sat on our bags by the side of the road where cows lumbered by and we waited for some kind of help.

And we sang while we waited, songs like "Boogie Woogie Bugle Boy" by the Andrews Sisters, and eventually an army jeep rolled up and a woman in uniform stepped out and said her name was Lieutenant Barbara John. She had a firm jaw and a deep voice, and she asked why we'd begun walking when she was supposed to pick us up?

We piled into the jeep feeling chastised and worn, and she asked us clipped questions as we drove to the base, like "Why do you want to serve our country?" and "Are you ready to watch men your age die?"

It was all very sobering and the sun was very hot, and by the time we'd reached the iron gates of the camp, all I wanted was to crawl into bed and fall asleep.

But there was no time for sleep at Camp Lee.

There was marching. We may not have had the same privileges as the men, but we got the same treatment. Dressed in helmets and boots, we went for long hikes carrying full field packs. And we practiced using our gas masks.

We shared bunks with ten other women, and we wore uniforms they gave us: a khaki greatcoat, barathea skirt and hip-length jacket, peak cap with a high crown, and a cap badge. Every morning we stepped into the darkness and marched, even as the sun rose.

I had never truly appreciated walking or even standing still, but now I did, as my knees ached and my head pounded and I couldn't complain about it to Eva who marched beside me, and I wondered, why do nurses need to know how to do this?

The corporal said something about discipline and valor, but all I could think about was rest and roast beef and how it seemed years since I'd had any of either.

Supper was always a fast affair in the dining hall with metal plates and piles of gelatinous stew or Spam on a bun and a square of chocolate wafer that was hard as a rock and tasted like bitter coffee. It was all supposed to prepare us for the army, but all I felt ready for was bed.

But bedtime didn't come.

Eight o'clock and the sirens and a voice over the loud speaker telling us to line up outside and march for another hour.

When it was finally over, I'm not sure I didn't fall asleep before I fell into bed; and then it was morning again.

More marching and then we were given cold slops of porridge and some very strong coffee, and we stood at attention as Commanding Officer Norma Crowe entered the room and saluted us.

"She's the head honcho," Eva said in a low voice, and Norma frowned at us and we didn't talk anymore.

"Welcome, ladies," she began. She had shiny hair pulled straight back into a bun, and it seemed to stretch her whole face tight. "The Army Nurse Corps is one of the most esteemed organizations. It requires diligence, determination, and compassion. You will be called upon at any moment to serve the most severe and complicated of injuries, and you will be forced to do battle on behalf of the soldiers who are risking their lives for us. Are you prepared to give of yourself in this manner? Do you have the Courage to Care? The Courage to Connect? The Courage to Change?"

I felt my blood rushing, and I yelled with all of the gusto my small form could give, "Yes, Ma'am," along with the rest of the girls and there was a passion in me I didn't know I had except, of course, for Jimmy Stewart and Humphrey Bogart. But this was a different matter entirely.

In the afternoon we learned the Nurse's Creed, and it's something etched across my heart to this day and it goes like this:

> I am a member of the Army Nursing Team.
> My patients depend on me and trust me to provide compassionate and proficient care always.
> I nurture the most helpless and vulnerable and offer courage and hope to those in despair.
> I protect the dignity of every individual put in my charge.
> I tend to the physical and psychological wounds of our Warriors and support the health, safety, and welfare of every retired Veteran.
> I am an advocate for family members who support and sustain their Soldier during times of War.
> It is a privilege to care for each of these individuals and I will always strive to be attentive

and respectful of their needs and honor their uniquely divine human spirit.

We are the Army Nursing Team.

We honor our professional practice standards and live the Soldier values.

We believe strength and resiliency in difficult times is the cornerstone of Army Nursing.

We embrace the diversity of our team and implicitly understand that we must maintain a unified, authentically positive culture and support each other's physical, social, and environmental well-being.

We have a collective responsibility to mentor and foster the professional growth of our newest Team members so they may mentor those who follow.

We remember those nursing professionals who came before us and honor their legacy, determination, and sacrifice.

We are fundamentally committed to provide exceptional care to past, present, and future generations who bravely defend and protect our Nation.

The Army Nursing Team: Courage to Care, Courage to Connect, Courage to Change.

That night we went to the officers' club. It was a square box of a building down the gravel road from camp, but it seemed like a castle compared to the warehouse we were in. I wore a dress Mama had made me for my seventeenth birthday with material from our living-room curtains. It had red roses on the fabric. I pinned up my hair and bit my lips and pinched my cheeks, and Eva and I giggled as we ran down the gravel road to the building all lit up like a kerosene lantern.

I had to forget I was a preacher's daughter. The place was wall to wall with couples and music and drinks, but the more we danced the easier it was to believe I was someone else.

The men were not so much gentlemen as guys our age, waiting to be called back to duty, so we all just kind of lingered together, dancing and listening to Ella Fitzgerald. "This is the life," Eva said, as the men escorted us back to our gate before curfew.

And suddenly, I looked down at my dress and pictured Mama standing at the kitchen window with an empty mug in her hand, and I couldn't breathe for a moment, wondering what on earth I'd done.

Then Johnny, the guy whose arm I was on, kissed me. And I didn't mind much what Mama was thinking anymore.

Nights, though, were hard. Under my thin green blanket in the dark of the barracks with women snoring around me, I cried into my flat pillow and wondered if God would ever forgive me. The Bible talks about honoring your parents, but how can you honor them when they're wrong? And I knew my Bible inside and out because it was the only book I'd ever been allowed to read in my house.

I could still hear them, the girls and boys skipping to school with their school bags, all linking arms, while I sat at our round kitchen table and Daddy preached at me, taught me about creation and the Tower of Babel and used those stories for science and English lessons. I had no friends, because we were meant to be *in* the world, not of it; so I sat in my room and played with my teddy bear and dreamt of having a girl to talk to.

Then there was the day when my bedroom window was wide open and the air smelled of honeysuckle, and there was someone singing to herself on the sidewalk below, and I climbed out my window and down the tree and landed right in front of her. Standing there in my frizzy red curls and my checkered pinafore, I stuck out my hand as I'd seen Daddy do at church and said, "Hi, I'm Clara. How do you do?"

This girl just looked at me with her wide green eyes and then swung her blonde hair back and laughed, and it was the prettiest laugh I'd ever heard. Kind of like a river trickling. And she shook my hand. "Nice to meet you, Clara. I'm Eva."

"Pleased to make your acquaintance," I said.

She laughed again, shook her head. "You're sure different. But it's all right. Come on, let's go play hopscotch."

I was nine years old when I met Eva, and she was my first friend, and Daddy didn't find out till I was eleven. It helped he was never home, always visiting this church person or another or trying to make new converts, and come schooltime every morning, precisely at nine o'clock, I made sure I was sitting at the kitchen table with my Bible, waiting, so he wouldn't wonder.

But Mama knew. She never said a word. Just smiled a little when she caught me climbing through my window and said, "Why don't you use the front door?"

Here I was, now, in a cold bunk room with ten other girls and Eva in the bed above me, and I knew her better than anyone else in the whole world. So why was I missing our tiny little kitchen with its flickering bulb and Daddy's tall broad shoulders? Why was I missing the humming refrigerator and Mama's toast and tea and the birds singing outside my bedroom window?

Daddy hadn't said much when he'd found Eva and me stargazing one night in the backyard after he thought I'd gone to bed, and suddenly there he was towering over us, smelling like toothpaste. I guess he'd gone in to kiss me good night and found me missing. He just kind of picked me up like I was little and slung me over his shoulder and turned around and went back inside, tossed me on my bed, and said not to leave again or I'd be sorry.

The next morning, he acted like nothing was wrong, which wasn't like him, only I think Mama might have stuck up for me in one of her rare moments of courage. And Eva and I, we just kind of kept hanging out.

Eva introduced me to the library, on Raymond Street, which was tucked right behind Daddy's church on Main, but I'd never seen it before. We spent hours in there, reading everything from *Pippi Longstocking* to *Anne of Green Gables* to *Nancy Drew*, and they were better than any Bible story. She took me to her house with its white pillars, at the far end of town near the wide open fields. Her daddy was the mayor, and her mama never had to cook or clean, she just had to throw parties and read magazines while sitting in wide sun hats and drinking lemonade. Their maid gave us strawberry milk shakes, and we sat on the back porch and listened to big band music on the radio.

I always went home for supper, and Mama would look at me sadly sometimes because she could tell I'd been having so much fun. I was flushed and shiny and never looked that way at home. I knew she wished she could be the kind of mother who could make me look that way. But I just wanted her to be her.

I would squeeze her hand and say, "Hello, Mama," and she'd squeeze mine back and say, "Hello, Clara," and we understood each other this way. The way that says, *You are perfect to me*.

Eva didn't go to church. She went to mass. Her daddy often traveled on the weekends, so she and her mother lit candles and spoke in liturgies and then went home for fried chicken and potatoes. We both spent the Sabbath on hard pews. I tried to get her to come to church with me, but she said Catholics and non-Catholics don't mix and I didn't understand this, because I thought we mixed quite well, except on Sundays.

So on the train ride to Virginia, we decided we wouldn't do church or mass anymore; we'd focus on loving people instead, and we weren't even sure God existed, because if God is good, then why would he allow Pearl Harbor and Hitler and our men to be shot in war?

We didn't know much about the Holocaust at the time, about the trainloads of Jews being deported from their homes and about the old and the sick being stuck in ovens while children starved and parents were enslaved. We didn't know. We knew about Hitler and his voice screaming through the radio and his funny moustache and his mass following. And I wonder now if I would have cared so much about the injustice of our men being killed in light of the greater injustice, of a nation of God's people being slaughtered. I'm pretty sure my heart would have changed.

But it wouldn't be until after the war that I'd learn the full extent of the atrocity, when a woman named Corrie ten Boom came and spoke to our church years later. It was then that I got it: the genocide, marked in the grooves of her face, and the way it had wiped out her family, and the extraordinary power of God's forgiveness shining through her.

But all I knew at the time, at the age of twenty, was my own little world. And as I lay shivering in my bunk under my green army blanket, the room full of drafts, I talked to God while women snored around me, and I begged his forgiveness because I knew in spite of the war he did exist. How else could I explain the warm, sacred place inside my heart, the place that told me that while angry fathers and sad mothers and hard pews were real, love was, too? And would one day prevail?

———— ✦ ————

The day was July 19, 1943. The day the Allies bombed Rome for the first time. The day we were told we were being shipped out. The day I received a telegram from home stating: "Return now or be disowned."

I wrote back, "Take care of Mama."

We were taken by train to Fort Dix, New Jersey, where we waited for the ship to take us somewhere overseas, somewhere far from a family I no longer had.

And as we waited, Eva and I just sort of clung to each other and I knew this was it. I was on my own. And for the first time in my life, I felt free.

Terrified.

But free.

4

I didn't know I could get this sick, and a boy in uniform held my hair as I threw up over the side of the ship as we tossed and turned over the North Atlantic on the USS *Mariposa*.

So much water. Eva didn't seem to notice. She was always laughing because we were six hundred nurses sharing the troop ship with a batch of baby-faced soldiers, and she said she wanted to have a good time. "Me, too," I told her, "But it's hard because, well, my face is green."

She patted my hand and made some kind of motherly clucking noises. Then she found me some club soda and crackers and left me in my bunk, in the belly of the ship.

I huddled there and cried a bit and wondered if all this was worth getting disowned for; but Timmy, the man who'd held my hair, kept me company a lot of times. We played cards— which Daddy would have frowned on—but not once did he try to get fresh with me. I found out later he had a crush on Eva. Every guy did. He didn't mention her much, though. He just lay on her bunk while she was gone, and me, on mine, and we talked about what we were going to miss about home.

He said he was going to miss his mama's homemade biscuits smothered in strawberry jam—"but we haven't had those in a long time, anyway," he said, sadly.

I was quiet for a while, trying to remember what biscuits tasted like. "I'm gonna miss libraries," I said, and he looked at me for a long time and then pulled out something from his back pocket. It was a well-worn copy of the Psalms, and he handed it to me. "Take this," he said. "My grandpapa gave this to me before I left. It's my favorite book from the Bible," and I paged through it, saw the brown stains on the edges from his thumbs, and shook my head. "Thank you, but no. I've had all the Scripture I can stand. My daddy, he's a preacher man," and I handed it back.

Then we were both quiet as the boat rocked, and I was almost asleep when, "I hear we get free cigs in the army!" Timmy said, his cheeks dimpling, and I wondered what it would be like to smoke. I'd never even had a sip of alcohol, and it was time, I decided. And then I ran down the corridor of the ship, ocean salt in my face, and threw up in the latrine because I was so scared of everything. Of the war, of the free cigarettes, of being alone with a boy in the belly of a ship. But he never once tried anything, and then, of course, I wondered if I was attractive at all because what boy wouldn't want to get fresh with a girl when he's going off to war?

"You were puking," Eva reminded me that night, her hair pinned up in curlers, dabbing lotion on her skin. "What guy would want to kiss a girl who's sick?"

"True," I said with a sigh, then I watched her pat her curls lovingly.

"I wish I could marry all of them," she said, and then we giggled. And I understood. There was something about leaving everything to make you want to hold onto something.

After six days at sea, they announced we were in France, docking at a port in Marseille, in a country at war and we all just stood there for a moment, on the deck of the ship, straightening our caps and jackets; and then the orders came, and we marched quietly off the ship, looking a lot like frightened children in a place far from home.

It was August 5, and yet, it was cold there by the water, and everywhere were Italian soldiers in their olive-drab uniforms and glaring swastikas, and I shivered a lot.

France had been occupied by Italy, and I didn't know it then, but the Germans would soon be taking over. On June 10, 1940, Benito Mussolini had declared war on France and Britain and the Italian army invaded France. I still remember Roosevelt's somber voice declaring, "On this tenth day of June, 1940, the hand that held the dagger has struck it into the back of its neighbor."

Then on June 25, 1940, after the Fall of France, an armistice was signed between France and Italy and the zone of occupation agreed upon, covering a scattering of small towns.

In November 1942, the area was increased, taking over many of the larger cities, and then Germany invaded, September 1943. One month after we arrived.

But we didn't know this. We only knew, at this moment, the Italians were everywhere, France was occupied, and we were protected by the Geneva Cross on our uniforms—the red Greek cross on a white background declaring all nurses neutral.

We were taken by a female commanding officer to an army train that made its winding way through fields of cows and thatch-roofed houses to a place called Normandy. And there weren't many trees. It's one thing I'll always remember; it all seemed so lonely, like the land had never been hugged.

Eva and I didn't laugh a lot on the train, and there was no sugar this time. We slept through much of it, piling off in haphazard form in Normandy where a kind-looking colonel greeted us.

She saluted us, and then we were taken in army trucks to the village where we were dropped off and escorted by other officers to various homes. Eva and I were paired together and placed in a two-story brick house, the home of a doctor and his wife and their baby, and they looked so warm and friendly, I could have fallen into their arms.

They took us to our room, which was small but clean with two canvas camp beds, two canvas buckets, a canvas wash-basin on a tripod, and a small square canvas bath.

After we'd washed up and eaten a meal of toast and beans and warm milk we were allowed to sleep, and even though it felt like it was all I'd been doing lately, I slept hard on the canvas bed. It could have been made of feathers it felt so soft, and I'm glad I slept well for the vision I beheld the next morning.

The field hospital was sixty tents holding twenty beds each. The heating in each tent was a small Beatrice oil stove. One blanket per bed.

Eva and I just looked at each other then looked at the ground and swallowed hard. Some of the beds were full of soldiers who ground their teeth or muttered or groaned. We were ordered to wash up and then report to our assigned tents. Eva volunteered to learn anesthesiology, but I wanted nothing to do with drugging people. I just wanted to make them feel less alone, so for the first time in years, we said good-bye. And even though I knew I'd see her again in eight hours, as she turned and walked away, it felt like the end of the world.

Yet, it wasn't. It wasn't the end of the world, because that happened when I looked into the faces of the soldiers and saw someone who reminded me of Timmy from the ship or the brother I never had and the pain only war could inflict: the pain of being so wrenched from reality you just toss and moan.

Eva and I were soon transferred from the doctor's house into tents in the middle of a cow pasture, where we had to wash our undergarments in our helmets. We coughed frequently because it was November, and there was snow on the ground, but all it took was looking into the eyes of a broken man to stop feeling sorry for myself. Most of the time.

During the fall and winter, there was pneumonia. There was pain in the legs, and then there were men who'd lost limbs and minds to the war, and in the beginning, when it was all fresh, many of us treated them with such dignity we got in trouble.

"Don't get too attached," the doctors said, but we were home to these men. They looked at us and saw their mothers, their wives, their sisters, and I didn't know what they'd witnessed on the front lines, but they saw angels in us. "Angels of Mercy," they called us.

But nights were still hard. At least I had Eva, and I wrote many letters to Mama, though my fingers shook so badly I'm not sure she could read them.

That is, if Daddy let her try to read them.

The letters went something like this: "Dear Mama, It's nearing Christmas and I can't stop thinking about your mincemeat pie. There are plans for those who have the day off to gather around in the recreation tent and sing carols and drink hot cocoa. We even decorated a fir tree with stars and candy canes cut from old plasma cans. We also hand-stitched seven hundred Christmas stockings from red jackets left behind by French soldiers who passed away. You would have been proud,

Mama, of how fast I sewed, my stitches so small and perfect. And we made four hundred pounds of peanut brittle and fudge with the help of our supplies officer, and we're going to hand out the stockings filled with goodies to each of the patients.

"But how I miss waking up in my red flannel pajamas and sneaking downstairs to find my stocking and emptying it before you and Daddy woke up. Those sweet mandarin oranges, those nuts, those dark chocolates you made by hand before everything was rationed. Then, listening to Daddy read the Christmas story and it was the one time I didn't mind the Bible. I can't imagine Christmas without that story. And always people over for dinner, for stuffed chicken and sweet yams and roast potatoes. You were so good about having people over who had nowhere else to go. I often thought they smelled, but you always treated them with such respect, and I'm trying to do that, too, Mama. I'm trying to love on these patients the way you loved on those guests. The way you loved on me. I love you, Mama."

I still actually wore flannel pajamas, most days—and nights—underneath my army uniform because I was so cold, and one evening in January I used the rest of my letter-paper to start a fire with our coal stove. And I all but burned down our tent.

Eva was gone; it was her day off and she'd taken the army jeep to the officers' club. She smoked now and drank gin, and I was still a good girl. I'm not sure why. I was scared, I guess, of enjoying myself too much when there was so much pain around me; but that night I drank some of Eva's gin and then poured the rest on the fire I'd started, and it caught the canvas tent on fire. I began smacking at it with my pillow, which promptly took flame itself.

The girls in the tent beside me smelled smoke and ran over. We were screaming and stomping on the fire, and then the snow finally killed it. And when Eva returned the next morning there was frost on our beds and a hole in our tent and she was none too pleased.

"Great golly, Clara, what were you thinking?!" she said, her hands flying up and she looked tired, like she hadn't slept, and my temper was as red as my hair.

"Well, maybe if you weren't off gallivanting with every man from here to kingdom come and cared a little more about why we are here, I wouldn't be in such a mess," I said, crossing my arms and feeling very much defeated.

She tossed her head, and it became apparent we were quickly growing apart. "I think you're jealous," she said, stepping across the coal bucket and the latrine pot and the bag with my clothes. She flopped on her bed and lay on her side and closed her eyes. "You're just jealous because I have a date next Saturday with a Frenchman."

I snorted and swung my legs over the side of my bed and pulled on my army boots and stomped to the tent door, which flapped noisily.

"You don't even speak French," I said, fumbling for the zipper of my jacket and pulling on my cap. "Anyway, I don't have time for dates. I'm here to serve my country."

And with that, I tried to slam the cloth door of the tent, which didn't work very well, and then I turned and marched off to my ward to begin changing beds while wiping at my eyes and cursing it all.

We didn't talk most of the week, and Eva went on her date that weekend and never came back. Later I learned she and the French soldier had fled in the middle of the night to elope.

My grade-school friend was gone, and I was more alone than I'd ever been, with only Miracle Martha to keep me company.

People called her that because she sang hymns wherever she went and made everyone feel better about themselves. Everyone but me. I found her annoying, with her cross necklace and her constant smile, and I didn't think anyone could truly be so happy. But for some reason she liked me, and on days off, she'd invite me to mass.

I'd always stammer and say I had something else to do, like go to the cinema. She'd nod and say, "Okay, maybe some other time." And I did go to the cinema because there's something religious about the way Clark Gable lights up a screen; but on the way home on the bus we'd pass through town, and sometimes I'd see the church aglow with candles and the stained-glass windows bright with color and I'd just weep and weep into my handkerchief, the one Mama sewed me last year for my birthday, my initials stitched in the corner.

And it went on like this for the next year, me just doing my job and caring for the soldiers, a few of them British, most of them French and American, and sitting in my canvas tent writing letters to Mama and going to the cinema on my days off. And eventually, Martha stopped inviting me to mass, and I was the red-headed girl who no one really knew.

And Mama's handkerchief got plain soaked through.

But then the Battle of the Bulge happened, and we were all too busy trying to keep the near-dead alive, we had no time to think about ourselves. And that's when I met Gareth.

5

I hadn't seen so much blood since D-Day.

Things had been kind of quiet since the Allies invaded France, since the morning of June 6, 1944, when fifty miles of Normandy's coast were occupied by Eisenhower and his troops, alongside the British, and the Germans never knew what hit them. We could still hear General Eisenhower's words through the static on the radio, his message to the members of the Allied forces, "You are about to embark upon the great crusade, toward which we have striven these many months."

And there was no denying the hell of those days. To look in our eyes would be to say we'd seen the devil. We were all moved down to the front lines, and the men, they came limping in, Germans leaning on Americans leaning on British, because one minute they'd been trying to kill each other and the next they were linking arms.

They were so confused. It had gone on too long, this vicious fighting, and for some of them, it didn't stop, not even when they were lying in their hospital beds. One man I tried to help knocked me into the next patient's bed while I was changing a dressing.

"You notice how they talk and talk, and they're so happy to be with American girls, and then they tell such awful stories and laugh and cry and then become deadly silent?" Martha said to me when we were breaking for three hours of sleep one night. "They're so damaged by it all."

I nodded. I could barely keep my head up, it felt so heavy. "Yeah, and then the Germans, some of them are so committed to the end. I had a guy die tonight with his hand raised, saying 'Heil Hitler.' Another guy refused a blood transfusion because he only wanted German blood, and we had none."

It was all so silly and frightening, and we'd finally fall asleep when the next ambulance would roll in with piles of wounded, some of them just a mess of flesh and blood. We'd rise and work quickly in the dark to get them stabilized and onto something that would float, then shipped off the beaches to a transport ship and back to England where they could be hospitalized.

Since then, though, it had been rather dull. We'd expected D-Day to end the war, but the Germans refused to give up. Kind of like a kid in a game of tug-of-war, who insists on gripping the rope even though he's being dragged across the ground. So Christmas happened again mid-December with everything frozen and the carol-sing led by Martha, her cheeks red like the cherries in Mama's fruitcake (back when we had such luxuries). We'd stopped decorating trees or making stockings like we did the first year. But there was a small gift exchange amongst us nurses, wrapping up whatever we could find in our tents or whatever we could make. I took some coal and sketched the Nativity on a piece of flat white rock I found. The girls marveled over it and made me feel pretty special, but then it was my turn to choose a gift and I unwrapped a Gideon's Bible. I immediately looked at Martha, who was grinning as though she'd saved me.

But the Battle of the Bulge interrupted our festivities, when the Germans took the Allies by surprise and men started pouring into our hospital tents. They didn't look much like men, though. They looked like a mother's worst nightmare.

The battle started December 16, when the sky was overcast. And even though the Americans and British were taken by surprise, the odds were in our favor, and Allied reinforcements and improving weather conditions, which allowed our armies to attack German forces and supply lines, sealed the win.

But in the dark of the tents, in air smelling of formaldehyde and rotting flesh and sweaty skin, it didn't feel like a win. By January 25, there were some eighty-nine thousand casualties, including nineteen thousand killed, and they said it was the bloodiest battle yet. We worked through numerous nights, the sky as black as the ink I used for Mama's letters, and we still didn't mend half of the bodies, the other half strewn across the ground because we had no more beds.

And all I could think as I bandaged and prayed was, *This is someone's boy. Someone's baby who once laughed and gurgled and rolled all fat, who learned how to crawl and walk and sing the ABCs, someone's prayed-for miracle lying bloodied and near dead on this hard, flat bed.*

And where was God?

I begged my fingers to minister as they washed and wrapped gauze, and I smiled if any of the soldiers looked at my face, but night and day and hours wore on, and men died because we couldn't reach them fast enough. Because no matter how bright the light inside you, if everything around you is oppressively dark, it begins to leak into your eyes, and eventually you either die or find a miracle.

And I found a miracle.

It was the fifth day of casualties, and we were all going a bit mad, what with the smells and the darkness and not having eaten properly in days. Because it felt wrong to take any time for ourselves when so many were dying. So we were growling under our breaths and dropping tools in the dirt and stepping on the men all piled up.

And just when I thought I would faint for how hard it was, a sweet tenor voice lifted me up, singing in the corner of the tent. It's a voice I can still hear to this day, and it sounded much like your grandfather's, Noah, and it was singing the only hymn I could stomach after all of the hypocrisy I'd witnessed: *Amazing grace, how sweet the sound, that saved a wretch like me; I once was lost, but now am found, was blind, but now I see.*

I turned and searched among the dying faces for the one singing, and his eyes met mine. He was one of the most injured. I'm not sure why he wasn't on a bed, but I later found out he was an American torn apart by a German sniper and had risked his life bringing news to a nearby camp. The sniper had hit him before he'd made it, but his approach had been enough to alert the French troops.

And now he was singing, semiconscious on the floor, and I quickly finished stitching up the man I'd been working on and rushed to find a place to put Gareth.

He told me about his wife as he lay on a mattress stained with other men's blood, and I was panicking. No one was coming to give him drugs—later I would discover we were out—and his wound infection was spreading. But he was so peaceful through it all, like his inner light was of a thousand men, and he kept smiling at me while I cleaned him up and apologized.

"You remind me of her," he told me in a raspy voice, and I held water to his lips then continued bandaging his wounds. He'd lost so much blood already, and his skin was parched and pulled, like my daddy's leather Bible cover, and yet he kept humming and talking about Mattie, his wife, and how they'd met at Moody Bible Institute in Illinois.

"She was the prettiest thing, in her ruffles and her hair all done up, and I barely passed my courses for thinking of her," he said as I stitched and his eyelids fluttered like a hummingbird's wings. "She was the dean's daughter. We weren't supposed to date the dean's daughter, but I couldn't help myself."

He laughed and then coughed, and I held my handkerchief to his mouth, and when I took it away it was covered in blood.

"We were going to change the world, her and I," he said, "me a poor preacher and her, all fired up for folks, and then the war happened and, well, we prayed and thought I should go."

I stopped midstitch and stared at this man no older than myself, and he, a preacher? In battle?

And my worlds collided—my daddy's theology against Gareth's—and it took a minute before I could breathe again.

"So, you think you can love Jesus and fight, too?" I said, as gently as possible, snipping the thread, and he looked at me with the most kindness I've ever seen on a dying man's face.

"Jesus called us to defend the least of these," he said, then coughed some more red on my mama's hankie.

I knew we were going to lose him, this man who might have been the truest Christian I'd ever met, and with everything in me I wanted to save him. I begged him to hold on and dodged the beds and soldiers clamoring for help and found the chief of surgeons whose eyes were red as poppies, and he followed me back to where Gareth lay, looked him over, shook his head, and said, "I'm sorry, son. Your infection has spread, and we're all out of medicine. We should have got to you sooner. Do you want a chaplain?"

Gareth took a minute. I could see him searching the ceiling for answers, and then he said, "You know, Doc, the chaplain is probably near wore out. I've got Jesus right close to me now, and he's all I need. And a piece of paper and a pen if you don't mind."

The doctor nodded, patted Gareth's hand, then said, "Clara here will take care of you, won't you, Clara?" And I knew I would if it was the last thing I did.

Because sometimes on earth we entertain angels.

I ran to my tent and grabbed the Gideon's Bible, which lay thick with dust beneath my cot, and a pen running low on ink. I ran back to the ward where Gareth lay with his eyes closed. I feared I was too late, but then he opened his eyes and smiled. "Thank you," he said. "You are so much like my Mattie. Have I told you this?"

Then I handed him the Bible, apologizing, saying this is all I've got, and he paused but a moment, then said, "What better way to write a letter than using God's Word to base it on?" and he tore out a page from the Psalms. He tried to write, using the Bible for support, but his fingers shook and his eyes kept closing, and finally he said in a whisper, "I'm so sorry—would you do it for me, Clara? While I dictate?"

So I sat there in a room full of death, the moon on the walls and Gareth's face turning gray, and I wrote for him, this letter, my cursive looping over the typed verses of Psalm 40:

My dearest Mattie,

I promised, four years ago, to always love and cherish you, and my darling, I haven't stopped thinking about you since the moment I arrived here. You were the one to keep me going. Your letters were my lifelines, and often before I went to bed I would kiss the ink of those letters, knowing your hands had written them, and . . .

I don't know how I'm going to get around in heaven without you. I'm afraid I'll get lost without you there to guide me, my sweet Mattie. You always took such good care of this dreamer.

Here his voice broke. He turned to the wall, and his whole body convulsed. I had to stop myself from breaking the pen. It was too horrible, too sad, but then he turned to me almost fiercely and finished the letter with:

> But you must take care of yourself, now, my Mattie, you must. I cannot stand the thought of you *not* having those children you always dreamed of, the ministry you wanted to share with me. Share it with someone else, sweet Mattie, and I will be applauding you from where I sit in heaven.
>
> I love you more than feeble words can express.

Yours always,
Gareth

He made me promise to deliver this letter in person, took my hand in his and begged me, gave me his address in New Orleans. I said I would, I would see to it Mattie knew his love for her, and he sighed so deep and then asked if I would sing to him.

So I sang him into heaven, my off-key voice warbling "Amazing Grace," and I didn't stop holding his hand until it turned cold.

It was the night I stopped sleeping.

It was also the night I began believing in God again with a kind of fervor. Because I'd met a man who preached both love and justice, and seeing the two combined gave me

45

tremendous hope—for a life beyond this one, the one Gareth was now entering.

But the fact that I had sent Gareth there, that I hadn't gotten to him sooner, that I could have saved him if I'd heard his singing sooner, if I'd stitched faster, if I'd . . . This was what kept me from sleeping.

Funny how one can become so aware of God and humanity in the same breath and how knowing one, in fact, feeds the other. So instead of sleeping I spent hours bent low beside my bed, in my pajamas, my knees pressed into the rivets of the ground, cows mooing lowly beyond the tents, me begging God for the light by which to stand, the light of forgiveness.

On our days off, Martha and I biked the curved roads of France.

We became friends shortly after Gareth died, and with Eva gone, too, I was sore alone. So we biked, come spring, as the war raged on. We biked on our days off to villages around Normandy, and we played with the children we found, spent time with women whose houses had been bombed, and bought crusty loaves of French bread to hand out and cheese and meat, and it felt good to be giving in this way. To be outside, in the countryside of rolling green, and to remember life beyond war.

I still couldn't sleep, but at least, when I was awake, I was alive.

Whenever I did sleep, which was an hour here, an hour there, it was fitful and the dreams were always the same: a soldier missing his eyes but singing like a meadowlark, and every time I tried to help him, he flew away on broken wings and kept singing and flying, and I couldn't catch him.

And then I found him flat on the road, his mouth still open in song, and I would wake up crying and spend the rest of the night on my knees.

But mornings brought Martha, and grace, and we read our Bibles at lunch. We read to the soldiers, and they would beg for more, saying it was better than Dickinson, better than Wordsworth, better than any sweet poetry they'd ever heard, those psalms.

I believed in grace for everyone but me. I believed it for the soldiers, whom I became passionate to save, and for every man whose hand I held as it turned cold, and I believed it for the villagers who gave Martha and me bouquets of wildflowers and whose children danced to our songs. But I couldn't believe it for myself.

Perhaps it had something to do with Mama never having loved herself. Or Daddy never really wanting to spend time with me.

I just didn't believe this frizzy-haired girl from Maryland was someone Jesus would have wanted to die for. But Martha seemed to think differently.

"Girl, your hair is the prettiest thing I've seen since my grandma's red tulips," she said one day as we biked along the Andelle River.

"Thanks," I said, touching it tentatively. "I'll trade it to you for a dime. I never did like it much."

We pulled over to an apple orchard, white with blossoms and smelling like honey, and spread out a picnic on an old army bedsheet, the picnic being Spam on toast and some canned oranges, and we prayed grace over the food and ate it wearily. We were so tired of Spam.

"Remember ice cream?" I said around a mouthful. "Remember ham and turkey and sausage? Remember corn on the cob and garden lettuce and fresh raspberries?"

"And chocolates," said Martha. "When I get to Nebraska, I'm going to eat me an entire box. Every day. Until I'm good and fat."

We laughed, then, because there had been talk of peace, rumors of the Germans tiring and the Jews—those still alive—beginning to fight back and the Allies only gaining in numbers and conquests. Mussolini had been captured and killed, and Hitler had committed suicide with his mistress, and truth was being leaked out about the concentration camps, transcending judgment and racism.

Justice is such a glorious sight for the downtrodden.

We lay beneath the blossoms after our picnic, and I asked Martha if she'd ever picked apples growing up, and she said very quietly, "No." Then I found out she'd lived in an apartment with her grandmother, her parents dead from tuberculosis when she was little, and it had been all they could do to keep the coal bucket filled and the electric company happy. "There were no apple orchards—just concrete," said Martha. "So I came here to France to earn money to take care of my grandma."

Her grandma had been the one to take her to church, Martha explained, and she was the kind of person to take your face in her strong hands and kiss your cheeks repeatedly and tell you how loved you were, how beautiful you were.

"She's why I believe," Martha said.

And I thought how lovely it would be to have a grandmother like that.

Then it was time to return to camp along the river, the spokes of our wheels glinting in the sun and down below the bridge, young boys, fishing.

And even though I was tired and self-condemning, I knew without a doubt God was in the air, in the light, in the sounds, and he was watching over me.

PART 2

PEACE

It isn't enough to talk about peace, one must believe in it. And it isn't enough to believe in it, one must work for it.

—*Eleanor Roosevelt*

6

The car was slowing now, and Clara paused in her story, pulled herself out of her past, dusted off the virtual shrapnel and blood and dirt, and saw Shane turned around in his seat looking at her and Oliver peering through the rearview mirror.

Clara suddenly realized how tired her voice was, how wrinkled her hands—the same ones that had bandaged and soothed—and how white her hair in the reflection of the window.

"How I do go on," she said, muttering, almost angry.

Noah touched her hand. "Grandma, don't stop . . . "

She turned to the young man with his father's eyes and his Nintendo tucked neatly away in his backpack. This boy, he would rather listen to a rambling old lady than play his nifty games?

She blushed a little as Oliver pulled over.

"What are we doing, Dad?" Shane said, repositioning himself.

Oliver sat hunched, as though tired. "There was a sign for a bathroom and a restaurant. I thought we could break for a bite to eat."

Clara smiled at his worried expression, knew he was breaking more for her than anything, and turned to look out the window at the landscape that stretched for miles. It was all over, she kept telling herself. The war was over.

"Sounds lovely," she said in a whisper.

They were nearing Richmond, Virginia, the sign said, the big one by a slew of stores all stacked like gray Duplo blocks, and Clara felt crowded.

She smoothed her maroon skirt and white blouse, patted her curls, and pinched her cheeks because she suddenly longed to look younger, and stepped out into the sunlight.

And there they were—her daughters and her granddaughters filing out of the fancy SUV and the men pulling up behind them, stepping out of a Mercedes-Benz. She wasn't sure how her and Oliver's simple values had grown children with expensive cars, but she didn't like it. Nevertheless, she stepped forward to embrace them all.

"Lula, Nellie!" she said, kissing her daughters on the cheeks. "How goes the trip? Are you bored yet? Is everyone doing okay?"

"Oh, Mama, you worrywart!" Lula's blue eyes teased her; she'd always looked a bit like Marilyn Monroe, Clara thought. She'd been anxious about her eldest daughter's good looks, about whether men would take advantage of her, but businessman Bobby O'Connor had proven worthy. Wealthy, but worthy. He and Lula always took in foster children in addition to their two girls. So it was hard to fault them.

Nellie hugged her and smiled gently. "We're doing well, Mama, and you? You look a bit tired." Nellie had her father's long nose and fingers and was the classical prodigy, the one who played piano at three and concerts at six and had married a conductor named Kent Jamieson. It wasn't uncommon for them to spend months at a time in Europe, playing in stained-glass cathedrals and concert halls.

"I'm fine," Clara said, turning to the grandchildren, and she could never stop from tearing up when she looked at them. Their faces and fingers and toes and their lengthening limbs, so radiant and perfect, and all of this from a woman who never expected to have children.

They clamored to her, and she touched their hair gently as though blessing them, and they laughed and told her stories about one another's antics, and they were all girls save for Noah.

How they loved their oldest cousin. He approached now, threw the youngest girls, Mia and Caitlyn, over his shoulders and said, "How did these two get here? I'm afraid I'll have to send them back. There's got to be a post office around here somewhere," and they squirmed and giggled in their curls and their pink summer dresses while the other kids laughed and ran after Noah.

Kent and Bobby were already comparing routes with Shane, talking about the shortcuts they could possibly take and pulling out their GPSs and Raspberries or BlackBerrys or whatever they were called. All of this technology made Clara tired, and she could remember when all they had was the telephone and the radio. She turned to find Oliver. He was with Beth, Shane's wife, who was walking with him to the bathroom. She was so good to him. She and Shane were the only ones Clara and Oliver truly felt akin to; it was their minivan Oliver was driving. Even though Beth and Shane had a couple of kids, they lived in a two-bedroom house, a parsonage, because Shane was the pastor of the Inner City Alliance Church in Baltimore.

There was one restaurant. It was run by a portly fellow in a fishing hat, and he led them to tables with red-checkered cloths and smudged glass bottles of ketchup and vinegar while the stereo played Willie Nelson. A woman came up shortly

53

after, handed out menus, which consisted of sandwiches and deep-fried foods, and asked what they wanted to drink. The kids ordered milk shakes, and the adults went with soda pops or water. Clara thought they made a fine tribe, stretched out along those checkered tablecloths.

Clara was sitting beside Oliver, and his arm shook a little as he held his menu, but it was an answer to prayer that he could even hold a menu with his prosthetic hand.

And after they'd ordered their meals of onion rings and burgers—all except Lula who always had a salad because she was watching her figure, she said—Clara cleared her throat and said, "We just wanted to thank you for making this trip with us," and heads swiveled. She looked at her glass of tap water. "It's been so long since we've been all together, so this means a lot to your father and me."

Nellie, who was sitting across from Clara, reached over and squeezed her hand. "I'm sorry we've been so busy lately, Mama. Work has been crazy, and we've been traveling so much with the orchestra. But with Mia starting school soon, we're going to try to settle down."

"That would be lovely, dear," Clara said. She looked over at four-year-old Mia who sat on Noah's lap. "And good for you for putting your daughter first. It's something we always tried to do with you children, put you first, but there's something I never told you."

It was very quiet now, while Clara swallowed, and Oliver said, "Do you want me to tell them, dear?"

"No, it's okay," she said. "I need to do this."

Then she found Shane's eyes and said softly, "You remember the story I told you, Shane, about your mother? About how she asked me to take care of you?"

He nodded and smiled at her. "Yes, and thank you again, Mama. I am so grateful for you and Daddy taking me in."

She shook her head. "That's not all, though. Before it happened, I didn't plan to become a mother. I never even wanted to get married because, well, I'd seen what it had done to women like Mattie."

"Gareth's wife?" Noah said.

"That's right, Noah."

And there came a clamoring of questions, and Oliver raised his prosthesis and said, "Let your mother explain. This is hard for her."

They all quieted because when Oliver spoke, it was slowly and solemnly, as though he was parting the Red Sea.

Clara patted Oliver's shoulder. "Thank you, honey."

She turned back to the expectant faces, none of them ever having seen war, and she felt like the bell that tolled.

"Mattie was the wife of a soldier I tended to, during the war," she said. "A soldier who helped me believe in God again after all of the death and sadness I'd seen. He died under my care," she said, fidgeting with her napkin, "but before he died he asked me to deliver a letter to his wife, Mattie. So I did. I took the letter to her, and she and I have remained friends to this day. You know, your Aunt Mattie? Well, we're going to be meeting up with her in Louisiana."

"Wonderful!" said Beth from where she sat at the far end beside Shane, their fingers touching. "Where exactly in Louisiana?"

"At the war museum we're planning on going to, which just opened in New Orleans," said Clara. She pulled a bag out from under the table and extracted a quilt the children knew well. It was a quilt they'd all been wrapped in, and Clara tenderly touched the names stitched into the cloth.

The patches of fabric were varying shades of blue and yellow, and next to her children's names there were others—fifty-seven others—and beneath each name, a promise, stitched in white. A word, written in tiny cursive, blessing the baby. The whole quilt covering a generation of children, blanketing them in hope.

"I never told you the full story behind this quilt. Mattie gave it to me, as a thank you, for delivering her husband's letter," said Clara. "It was a baby blanket she'd sewn, in hopes of having children with Gareth one day. She doesn't know it, but this quilt has been accepted by the curator of the museum as an artifact. We have a deadline to get it to him—by Friday of this week. If we meet the deadline, it will hang as a permanent fixture. I'm not sure what Mattie's response will be, but I'm hoping it will be a good one. You see, I want to give back to her. For the way she helped me to forgive myself. For the way this woman, who lost her husband, helped me find a reason to live. And for how she led me to eventually have a family of my own."

Clara paused, because her heart was tiring and sore, and she looked around the table and said, quietly, "If it wasn't for Mattie, I would never have found my way to your father nor to each of you. So in a way, this trip is about commemorating the gift of friendship. The gift of family. The gift of faith. And it all started with a quilt."

7

May 1945

We were in Marseille the day it happened. VE Day.

Martha and I were waiting at the train station because the Germans had taken over and our tent-city hospital torn down, and we were asked if we wanted to work for the opposing army or be sent to the CBI (the China Burma India Theatre), a name given by the US to the forces operating alongside the British and Chinese Allied air and land forces in China, Burma, and India.

We told them we wanted neither. I wanted to go home and take piano lessons, and Martha wanted to take tap. So they sent us to the CBI.

The day they gave us our orders, we sat at the train station, watching the wind kick up the dust on the tracks and the sky brim brazen with light. The place was strangely still, as though an empty vase waiting to be filled and then, static through the radio, which had been playing Debussy, and an announcement made in breathless French, then German, then Dutch, then English.

Berlin had been captured by Soviet and Polish troops and the Germans surrendered. The war was won!

May 8, 1945—a date we'll always remember. After six years of slaughter and sorrow, the earth still rotated. And the war was over.

And all we could do was sit and stare at the tips of our dusty army boots peeking out from beneath our dirty, frayed skirts and wonder if we weren't dreaming. I'd imagined this moment so often it didn't seem real, but then we heard the sound of the masses cheering over the radio, and later it would be said all of Europe went wild, nurses joining men and women and children in the streets, everyone hugging and kissing like they were family. Because when you're fighting for your life, all of humanity becomes one desperate body. And Martha and I looked up to find each other and to hug each other and to do a little dance right there in the middle of the empty station.

"We're going home!" we sang.

The words tasted as sweet as fresh fruit, something we would experience again in days to come. Fruit and chocolate and showers and mattresses and perfume and lipstick and pretty dresses.

And steak. I couldn't stop thinking about having myself a good slab of steak.

After we danced, we waited for a train to come, squealing and laughing, and we rode it to the army ship as planned, but instead of heading to the CBI, we headed west, across the Atlantic.

Home.

And I swore I could see Lady Liberty herself, waving.

———

It was on the ship amongst the celebration of soldiers and nurses that I remembered.

I had no home.

I had been disowned.

I quietly put down my glass of champagne and nodded to the man who was talking about capturing a German in the basement of an abandoned house the day the Axis surrendered, and I slipped downstairs to Martha's and my room and sat on the bunk and cried.

What had I been thinking?

Mama hadn't responded to any of my letters. No doubt Daddy hadn't let her read them. He'd probably burned them, or maybe he'd used them as sermon illustrations.

It had been so long since I'd let myself think of home, for every time it brought me to tears and I hated crying. I felt weak when I cried, but it was all I could do now. And so, for a while, I soaked my pillowcase, and then I got angry. Angry at how Daddy didn't know the truth about the war, how he just stood at his pulpit and spouted about peace while men died to make it happen. Five hundred thousand men from the United States alone had died to make it happen.

And news had just started to leak about the concentration camps. Even on the ship, we learned more, about how the Russians were the first to discover the camps where Nazis had sent Jews and anyone else deemed undesirable, and how hundreds of thousands of prisoners had been forced to work for the Nazis under brutal conditions and on very little food. Some of the nurses on the ship had been sent there to care for the prisoners, including a girl named Vera Rieck. She was part of the 95th Evacuation Hospital who helped care for the thirty thousand at Dachau, a camp near Munich. "To see those poor, starving people," she said. "It was very, very, very sad."

She told us how, before entering the gates, she'd been sprayed with DDT to ward off lice and disease, and inside they'd found emaciated people—walking skeletons carrying tuberculosis, typhus, lice, and dysentery. In some places, other nurses had said, you could see hands sticking out from the ground, the dead piled in heaps around the camp, and the living too weak to bury them. And when they were finally freed, some of them died from eating too fast, they were so hungry and starved.

Approximately ten million people died in those camps, and more than six million of those were Jews.

And so I lay there on my bunk feeling angry at it all, at the injustice of it all, and then I fell into a fitful sleep—it was the first I'd really slept in days—and in it, I was standing in front of the diner.

In my dream, I somehow climbed up the side of my house in my uniform and crawled through my bedroom window and stood in a room not my own. The bare walls had been plastered in flowered paper, and the bed was ruffled in pink sheets, and a little girl with blonde curls was sitting on the floor having a tea party with my dolls and my teddy bears. I tried to say something, but I couldn't.

Then the door opened, and Daddy entered. He didn't see me; he just saw the little girl and went to her and picked her up and twirled her around and kissed her cheeks. "How's my sweetheart?" he said. "I missed you today." She giggled and held onto his neck.

Through the crack of the door I saw Mama, and she was sitting in her rocking chair like she always did, and she saw me, too, and she cradled her arms like she was holding an invisible baby and kept rocking, rocking.

And all I could do was watch silently. When I tried to walk toward her, my feet stuck to the floor, and then Daddy saw me. He saw me, and his face turned into a pickled beet, and he pulled all of my letters out of his shirt pocket and threw them at me, yelling, "Get out! Get out of my house!"

And I turned and fell out of the window and woke up in a cold sweat.

It was dark now, and Martha was standing over me, a shadow against the moonlit hall of the ship in her cotton nightgown, and the air smelled like saltwater. And then I realized my cheeks were wet from crying, and I was smelling my own sadness.

Martha sat down beside me and said, "Are you okay? You were sobbing in your sleep."

I wiped at my cheeks, realizing I was angrier at myself than anyone. Angry again at how I'd let myself down. At how I'd let Gareth down. At how I'd let my parents down. And wondering if I'd ever be able to do right.

I tried to explain it all to this wonderfully simple girl whose life was love and God and faith. Whose hair was carefree, blown brown around her round, kind face; but all I wanted was to be alone.

And after trying to convince me I was not a failure, that I was, indeed, very much adored, Martha left me alone while I got out of bed and went to stand at the railing of the ship. To stare up at the skies as we glided by, to hear the wash of the waves against the side of the boat and to know in spite of all my fears, the world, and God, were bigger.

So I practiced trusting in that moment. I practiced letting go and believing somehow, good would come out of it all, in spite of having no address, no family, and no future.

The shore was a loving sight, after a week at sea.

We docked at New York Harbor, our sixteen-story army vessel, and it took two hours for everyone to unload. And even after Martha and I had descended onto dry land, I could still feel the boat rocking beneath me.

All around us were people who spoke English. For a while we just walked, gripping our torn satchels and dressed in the only civilian clothes we had—two very faded dresses, desperately out of style—but we were home. In a land selling bananas and oranges, we bought bunches of them and peeled them like they were treasures and ate the sweet fruit until we felt sick.

Taxis and delivery trucks were bumper to bumper, and VE Day still hadn't hit the city; it wouldn't until August, when President Harry Truman's voice announced victory against the Japanese.

Until then, many men were still missing, and the ones who stumbled around us looked lost as well. Later we'd realize it was Soldier's Heart, or battle fatigue. For now, victory was just a word. The whole world was still reeling from its loss.

We ate at a little restaurant crowded with women and children, and the women looked like they hadn't slept, and the children were skinny and dirty. War still ravaged here, we realized, in the hearts and minds of those who waited for their husbands and fathers.

We ate fish, fresh from the sea, and we ate it slowly, savoring it. Then we found a hotel, and Martha fell asleep right away, while I lay there, fighting the waves rocking within me and rereading Gareth's letter to Mattie.

The next day, Martha would take the train home to Nebraska to see her grandmother.

"Come with me," she'd said at supper, wiping fried-potato grease from her fingers with a paper napkin. "My grandma would love to meet you, and you can find a job in our town and stay with us for a while until you figure out what you want to do."

I hadn't answered right away. I'd wanted to go with her. I'd wanted to know this grandmother and to have a house to live in, to feel like I belonged.

But I also knew the longer I prolonged being on my own, or visiting Mattie and giving her the letter, or returning home and asking forgiveness, the harder it would be later; so I said good-bye to Martha the next day. We prayed together at the train station in our dresses that we'd scrubbed in the hotel sink the night before and hung in the window to dry.

Then I watched the train leave and her waving and me standing on the platform, the train getting smaller and smaller, until we both just kind of disappeared.

It was a twenty-hour trip from New York to New Orleans where Mattie lived, so I decided to spend some of my army wages on a new dress. I hadn't shopped in years and wasn't sure I remembered how to do it. I walked the streets of New York, all grimy from car soot, until I found a fabric store. The women there helped me pick out yards of yellow cotton because it was summertime and I wanted to feel bright and happy.

I spent the next two days in New York City while a seamstress made my dress, and I soaked in the tub in my hotel room for hours, reading magazines and eating mangoes and bananas and oranges and strawberries by the bushel.

I felt very much like a new woman, except for the insomnia. Every night, war still raged in my head, and when I finally drifted to sleep, it was either my daddy yelling at me or the soldier with no eyes and the meadowlark voice, so I almost preferred not sleeping. These restless nights were beginning to wear on me, and my skin was as pale as the hotel sheets.

When my yellow dress was delivered to my room, I climbed out of the bathtub, threw out my old army fatigues, wore my new outfit downtown, and entered a department store. I purchased some lipstick, a sun hat, a pair of slacks, a blouse, a silk nightgown, and a new satchel to carry it all in.

Then I took the taxi to the station and bought a ticket to New Orleans.

The train was new and full of soldiers returning home, looking ambushed and excited at the same time.

I had a seat to myself, and I stared out the window much of the time. At one of our stops, I willed myself to walk to a phone and dial the operator and ask to make a long-distance call to a Mrs. Marie Wilson. When that didn't work, I sighed and trembled as I asked for a Reverend Clarence Wilson.

She patched me through, and Daddy's voice came on. The operator asked if he would accept the charges, and without a pause, he said, "Yes," and I didn't know what to think.

"Clara," he said then. "Is it really you? Are you there? Are you okay?"

"Yes, Daddy, I'm here," I said. "I'm okay."

"Your mother and I, we've been so worried," he said, and then the train conductor called, and I said, "I'm sorry, I have to go—I will call you soon." He said, "Don't wait too long."

And I couldn't even say anything for being all shaken up. I just hung up and stood there until the train whistle blew, and then I ran down the track and leapt on in a most unladylike fashion and collapsed in my seat, like a wrinkled patch of sunshine.

8

Fields of cotton and sugarcane and rice stitched up the countryside, making colorful squares outside my train window.

I dozed in and out, my feathered hat in my lap and the soldiers around me trying to strike up conversations. We were all kind of numb and childlike, not knowing how to act without war raging around us, and it was so quiet. No airplanes roaring above us, no ambulance sirens or sounds of dying, no groaning or screaming or weeping.

Just silence. And I felt I could hold it, like a teacup.

The soldiers tried to strike up a conversation, saying, "Hey, pretty lady, where you going?" I smiled at their words and their boyish desperation. I wove in and out of sleep, and it was light and then dark. Then I saw the Mississippi River and knew I was almost there, and I hadn't even rehearsed what I was going to say.

Mattie would have learned that Gareth was gone. A telegram would have told her months ago, and my job, I supposed, was to fill in the gaps.

Yet how does one tell a grieving widow about a love only she can know?

I felt like an imposter and a criminal. By letting him die, by letting hundreds of soldiers die whose lives were in my care, I had essentially killed him. Them. How could she, how could any of the wives, sisters, or mothers, forgive me?

Even now my palms were sweating and Daddy had been right, all along. I was no better than anyone. I was a sinner, and here I'd gone to war thinking I could save people.

I reached inside my satchel for the letter—tucked within a pocket—and I pulled it out for strength, for a vision bigger than myself, for a picture of Gareth and his dying request. So I read his words inscribed by my shaky handwriting, slanted and curled, and leaned back, remembered him singing in the darkness of a tent filled with sick and dying men.

I remembered "Amazing Grace," and it sounded as sweet now as it had then. I remembered him needing only pen and paper because Jesus was with him, and I wondered what it was like to know heaven so close, to know God was with me. I opened my eyes then and saw weary men collapsed around me, and I wondered if joy truly came with the morning.

We pulled into New Orleans at two in the afternoon on Saturday, June 2. No one met me at the station because no one knew I was there.

All I had was Mattie's address scribbled on crinkled prescription paper. I held it and my satchel and searched the station for someone who could guide me to 24 Madison Lane.

There was a line of taxis outside of the station, stretched like one of those caterpillars I put in a jar as a child. I was six years old back when I picked twigs with leaves and put them in jars with my caterpillars. The jars sat on my bedroom dresser and those caterpillars were my friends—my only friends until Eva. I would greet them in the morning, all three of them, and say good night to them. Then they went to sleep in thick blankets Mama called cocoons, and two weeks later I awoke and saw they had turned into butterflies. I opened the jars because it seemed crowded in there, and those butterflies found the window.

Flew away.

Their wings all bright and shiny.

I climbed into a taxi, and we drove past men in bowler hats and suits and cars, so many cars, and women on bicycles and tall buildings and bands playing in corner cafes. Even though the war had just ended, I felt the country was shedding its cocoon.

The driver was black, an older man with white hair, and every once in a while he'd drum his fingers on the steering wheel and move his head, keeping time with jazz music on the radio.

We drove out of the city along the Mississippi River, where boats floated like lazy ducks, and down River Road, with its pillared plantations and rows and rows of cotton, like something out of *Gone with the Wind*.

And then, a side road and a hamlet with a small white church and next, a gravel driveway leading to an even smaller house with dahlias lining the walk, their heads heavy with petals.

A woman was bowed low over the petals, her hands in the dirt, as I stepped from the taxi, and she turned.

She smiled, as though she knew me.

"Why hello, dahlin'," she said in a southern accent, her face, a heart with a smile dimpling her cheeks. Hair, tied in a messy brown bun. And she did not look like a widow.

"I'm Mattie," she said. "How can I help you?"

She was walking toward me, wiping her hands on her apron, and she stood four inches over my five-foot-two.

"Hi," I said, rooted to the ground and swallowing. "I'm, well, my name is Clara, and I . . . well, I've come to . . . I was . . ."

Mattie laughed and put a hand on my arm. "It's okay, honey, I'm not going to bite." She was young, but there was a knowing to her. In the corners of her eyes, like rivers.

I took a deep breath. "Sorry. I'm nervous. You see, I was your husband's nurse before he . . . well, before he passed away."

She stopped laughing.

I reached inside my satchel for the letter and handed it to her. "He asked me to give this to you, Mattie."

It took a minute for her to grab the letter. A cat pawed softly down the walk toward us, rubbing against Mattie's ankles, and she shook her head.

"Thank you," she said, fumbling with the paper. "Won't you come in, Clara?"

She was looking down at the letter as she said it.

"Oh, I couldn't . . ." I began, but then her eyes lifted.

"Please," she said softly. "You were the last one to speak to my Gareth. Please."

I nodded, ashamed of my fear. "Of course. I'm sorry. I would love to."

And we walked toward the house, the cat winding between our legs, the flowers bowed low.

Mattie's home reached out like an old friend, with its shutters around the windows and its welcome mat and white lace at the windows. The kitchen was wallpapered with green and white checks, and there were plants on the windowsill.

"I'm trying to grow herbs," Mattie said, gesturing at the pots. "Some parsley, sage, and chives—do you cook?"

But she was still looking at the letter, and I mumbled something about not being very good at it.

In the living room there was a sewing machine with yards of fabric and spools of thread in a basket.

"Do you sew?" I said, trying to fill the silence, and Mattie nodded.

"I'm learning. I prefer to play music though," and I saw the piano, then, next to the fireplace.

Down the hall was a bathroom, small with rosebud paper, and then stairs leading up to a trio of rooms: a guest room, what seemed like an unfinished nursery, and a master bedroom.

I lingered at the latter, at the double bed with its quilt and the books piled on either side.

I saw C. S. Lewis's *The Problem of Pain* and *The Holy Bible*.

"Have you read C. S. Lewis?" she said, following my gaze, crossing the room, and picking up the paperback.

I shook my head. "Should I?"

"He was Gareth's favorite," she said. "He was reading it when he decided to enlist. I haven't been able to bring myself to read it."

She set it down beside a man's pair of reading glasses. "I guess it sounds pretty trivial."

"The book took your husband away from you. You're grieving. It's anything but trivial."

We turned toward the stairs and paused by the smaller bedroom, the one that seemed a nursery with a crib and soft cream wallpaper. There was a quilt draped over the side of the chair, with blue and yellow patches, tiny white flowers, and navy trim.

"Do you quilt, then?" I said.

"I try."

And we went downstairs.

She poured us glasses of iced tea with lemon.

The air smelled like lilacs, and out back, past the screen door that swung behind us, I saw a lilac bush whose blossoms were falling, purple rain.

We sat on the back porch in rocking chairs. Chickens clucking in a wire-mesh coop, the wind in the poplars, and Mattie's cat curled, purring—it was enough to put me to sleep, this rocking and quiet. But I could see by Mattie's eyes I should stay awake.

I was her last link. I had witnessed Gareth's journey from this world to the next and it seemed near adulterous that I should have shared such intimacy with a man only she'd vowed to know, but there was no malice in her. Only quiet surrender.

I set my glass down and leaned forward. "I've never met a man so in love," I said, and her eyes filled.

"From the moment I met Gareth, he talked about you," and I didn't tell her how he'd said I reminded him of her.

Now, being here next to her, in my red frizzy hair and yellow dress, I was unsure of our similarities, but he'd been a dying man. In the end, we all kind of look the same: like people, with flaws and hopes and loves and dreams.

"What did he say, exactly?" she said. "Can you remember his words?"

"He said you were beautiful, and lovely, and he couldn't get a pen and paper fast enough to write you a letter." I swallowed. "When we asked him if he wanted a chaplain, he said no, because Jesus was with him, but could he write you a letter before he died. It was his final wish."

She nodded slowly, her hair falling from its bun like a veil. "That sounds like Gareth. It was always Jesus first, then me, then his job, and it's the way it should be. I guess it's why he went to war, because he thought Jesus would have done the same, in his own way, sticking up for the mistreated and hurting, that sort of thing."

We waited for a while in silence, waited for some kind of sign or gift or offering, but there was only laughter in the leaves, the purring of the cat, the clucking of the chickens.

"I'm so sorry," I said. It sounded trite. "I wish . . ."

"It's okay," she said, but she was crying.

And we rocked.

What else does one do?

"Who preached while Gareth was gone?" I said eventually, picking up my glass.

"They've hired someone from town," she said, "an older gentleman, and he's quite good. Not as good as my Gareth, but he's older and wise. I'm working for the New Orleans Municipal Library now, and it's good for me, you know. All of those books." She laughed. "They're like old friends, not judging you and whatnot. They just kind of sit quietly and let you be in your own time."

She tried to smile, but her face fell into her hands and her whole body shook. I bowed with her, and she wiped her eyes with the ends of her apron. "There. It's done. Now, no more of this," she said to herself.

Turning to me, then. "You must take the quilt. I've decided."

I was quiet. She rose and returned with the quilt I'd seen draped in the nursery. "We were newly married when he left," she said. "And hoping to start a family when he returned."

I didn't know what to say. She handed the quilt to me, and I pressed my face into the folds. "Your child would have been so warm," I managed. "But . . . I don't have any children. And what about you? You're so young, I'm sure you'll still . . ."

She didn't let me finish. "No, I don't think so. I know this sounds strange but Gareth was the one. I can't imagine . . . at least not right now . . . And it's too hard. Staring at it all the time, wondering—it makes me sort of bitter."

Mattie swallowed. "Besides, I'm moving."

I looked around at the chickens and the poplars. Her chair was creaking, and I wondered how anyone could move from this kind of peace. "It isn't the same anymore," she said, seeing my eyes. "Not without him. It's kind of like a window, like I'm looking through but not able to get there, because he was my door. You know? So I'm just gonna move and start over."

"Where would you go?" I said, turning the quilt in my hands.

"There's a place close to the library. Just a small place, but it's better for me now."

She nodded. "Yes, I'm quite sure of it. You take the quilt. So you'll always remember us. So you'll always remember him, and maybe pray for me?"

I promised her right then to pray.

When we were done, we sat some more in the afternoon light and she said I could stay the night, but I thought perhaps I should go, remembering the way Daddy had said he missed me, how kind his voice had sounded. I wanted to walk into that kindness.

So we said good-bye at the end of Mattie's flower-walk, and I stepped into a taxi she'd called for me, her quilt in my satchel, and Gareth's note in her hands.

The world humming "Amazing Grace," even as the taxi pulled away.

9

Nothing had changed.

Nothing except everything about my childhood home of Smithers, Maryland.

I rode those long sixteen-and-a-half hours, the same hours we're driving now, only in reverse, and in a train, and I couldn't keep my eyes open; so I slept. It was as though my body had been waiting to meet with Mattie, and now I was catching up on months of sleepless nights.

So there I sat slumped over in my wrinkled dress like a wilted carnation. Mama had given me a bouquet of carnations for graduating nursing school, and I wondered if they still sat in my room in their vase, all dried out like the way I felt now.

And I wondered what Daddy would say when I showed up looking this way. Would he say, "I told you so. Sin always makes a person look sick and tired." Or would he gather me up in his arms as he had never done? Would he say, "I'm sorry, I'm sorry, I'm sorry"?

I laughed, even with my eyes shut, at the thought. Daddy had never even given me a full hug. Sometimes a side one. At most he kissed me on the cheek in the morning. As though afraid to get too close.

Mama would hug me gently like she didn't want to crush me, and I suddenly missed her with an ache so sharp I nearly sobbed.

And then we arrived in the town I'd grown up in, the town that had one little grocer, a post office, and Flynn's Drugs with its green vinyl stools and marble-topped soda fountain, where Eva and I used to slurp Green Rivers and make eyes at local boys. I would go there when Mama asked me to pick up her nerve medicine, and one day a boy noticed. A boy named Henry took me to Flynn's on my first date at sixteen. He bought me a chocolate malt using his paper route money. But Daddy didn't let me keep seeing him because he didn't go to our church.

"We don't date Catholics," he said as though both he and I were dating Henry. I didn't see why it made a difference. Catholic or Protestant, Henry still looked like a dream, but it didn't go far with Daddy, and he said if we continued, I wouldn't be allowed outside for a month.

So I told Henry I couldn't meet him at Flynn's anymore, and that night he met me at the bottom of the diner and we sneaked off to the water tower and kissed at the top.

Daddy never found out.

Then September came, and Henry went to college in New York City to become a big designer, and he said he'd come back and get me when he was rich. I never heard from him again, but it sure had been fun, kissing him on top of the world.

I could see all of Smithers from up there: the trellis in the town center, overgrown with ivy where big brass bands played every Fourth of July. The steeples of two churches—Daddy's, and Sacred Heart Catholic Church—as well as the roofs of three barbershops and McKinley's shoes.

And in twenty years nothing had changed; but as I walked down Main Street trying to flatten my hair and smooth out my dress, I stopped just short of the diner to find it reopened. I smelled burgers and fries and saw townspeople, mostly women and children, at every table.

I knew war had filled the restaurants because there was no food at home and women were just too tired from working to cook as well, but even our old diner?

The faded siding had received a fresh coat of paint, and freckled noses were pressed against the glass where "Smithers Family Restaurant" had been painted, and I hurried up the stairs that led to our house. Away from their view.

It wasn't until I reached the top of the stairs that I realized how damp my palms were, and I gripped the handle of my bag and prayed, *Help, help, help,* until I felt strong enough to knock on the door.

Daddy's sure footsteps were crossing the linoleum, then the lock turned, and there he stood in the same checkered dress shirt he always wore, the one with the missing button and the yellow stains under his armpits. He'd put a safety pin where Mama had always said she'd repair it. Mama was always forgetting things, and Daddy cared too little about clothing to remind her.

For a minute, we just stared at each other, and Daddy cleared his throat and said, "Clara," and stepped forward and took my satchel. "Welcome home."

I followed him silently, and the sun lit up our house. I felt like God was blessing us, until I saw Mama on her rocking chair, and then I stopped thinking about God or any kind of goodness completely.

She looked as though she'd aged a thousand years. Like she hadn't eaten in just as long, and her arms sat limply in her lap as she stared straight ahead, her green sweater hanging off her thin shoulders.

"She stopped talking the day you left," Daddy said behind me. "I've tried everything, but she just sits in her chair all day long and won't move."

He stepped toward Mama and put a hand on her shoulder. I'd never seen him touch anyone so gently. "Marie, Clara has come home. Would you like to say hi to her?"

Mama looked at him with such blankness I wanted to scream, but instead I stepped forward, too, and knelt down and took her hands in mine. "Mama, I'm home. Can you hear me?"

She turned her eyes on me, and all I saw was sadness. Such incomprehensible sadness, it was as though she'd been on the front lines, herself.

"Clara Anne," she said in a hoarse whisper. Then she patted my hands awkwardly, and her touch was cold.

She nodded and said, "Clarence, I'm tired."

And he wrapped her arms around his neck and picked her up like she was a baby, and she leaned her head against his chest as he carried her to bed.

I sat on the rocking chair and cried until I was wrung out.

Daddy came out awhile later and didn't say anything about my face, about the tears dried there, and for once I was glad. He just said, "Can I make you some tea?"

"Yes," I said, "I would love some," and my shoulders began to shake again, and he turned toward the kitchen.

How the roles had reversed, I thought, as the kettle whistled on the gas stove and even though it was June, I shivered. I wrapped myself in one of Mama's afghans and sat on the love seat, staring up at the mantel above the fireplace. At the black-and-white photos we'd taken over the years, of Mama, Daddy, and me.

There were five of them, one from when I was seven at the coast; we'd taken the train there for the summer, and Daddy had sat with his books on a lawn chair while Mama and I hunted for seashells. Daddy looked serious in the photo, like always, but Mama looked happy, one hand on her wide-brim hat to keep it from blowing away, her other hand around me and us laughing into the wind. I'd never realized how pretty she was. I always felt famous when we hired a photographer. Even though it took so long and we had to stand so still, it was worth it just to see Mama smile, but as the years wore on there wasn't so much laughing. Mama looked graver in each photo until the last one, when she even looked a little sad. Her arms were wrapped around herself and me, holding my hands in front of me, and Daddy, too, and us all seeming like we were trying to keep from falling apart.

Daddy brought me tea on a tray, with two cubes of sugar, which was a treat. Even though the war had ended, ration stamps had not, and we all begged for the day when we could again eat sweets in abundance.

"I'm sorry, I know it's not how your mother does it," he said, placing the tray in front of me on the footstool, "but it's the best I could do. Do you take sugar? Milk?"

"It looks wonderful, Daddy," I said, picking up the teacup and putting in the sugar. They made such delicious "plunks" in the water, and it had been so long.

Daddy sat down opposite me, on Mama's chair, and twisted his wedding ring. "I know you're not used to seeing your mother this way. I'm sorry you had to come home to this, Clara. I should have warned you . . ."

I shook my head. I could see how tormented he was. How gray his hair. The few strands remaining.

"It's okay, Daddy."

Then I noticed the stack of letters sitting, unopened, by Mama's chair. "She got my letters, then," I said, nodding.

Daddy nodded. "Yes, I gave them all to her, but she didn't open them. She's not doing much of anything these days. When you left, well, she just kind of . . . stopped."

I wasn't sure if he was trying to make me feel guilty but I did, and I didn't know how to process it, so I just drank my tea and he removed his glasses and rubbed his eyes. "It's not your fault. It's my fault," he said.

I set my teacup down.

"She blamed me for driving you away. And I've tried everything. I spend every day here with her, except Sundays. I cook her meals, bathe her, read to her, carry her to bed. But she's stopped talking and responding, and the doctors don't know what to do. They say she's given up, and how do you prescribe the will to live?"

I pulled at the yarn in the afghan and thought about Daddy caring for Mama this way. How I'd never even seen them hold hands, and now he was bathing her.

He jumped to his feet as though nervous. "I should get you something to eat. You must be hungry."

I protested, but he went to the kitchen anyway, rummaged around for a while, and came back with a piece of toast and a fried egg. "Will this do?" he said.

I swallowed. "It will do just fine, Daddy, thank you."

We both sat in silence while I ate and I was glad. Outside I heard the sound of children emerging from the diner and running down the street, automobiles driving by, and the occasional bicycle. I could see Mama's slim form lying in bed under a pile of blankets, and I could barely eat for it all: for Daddy, being so kind, and Mama, being so sick, and even the diner being open, and I wasn't good with change.

My bedroom looked the same as it had since I was a girl. I guess it's why the army was such a big thing for all of us, because we weren't used to change. "I'm sorry," I said, now, setting down my empty plate. "I'm so sorry I disobeyed you and made Mama get so sick."

"Clara, I'm the one who's sorry. I behaved wrongly. I shouldn't have tried to control you. It's just . . . well . . ." Here he looked down and I could see his jaw working. "I didn't want to lose you, too . . ."

My eyes widened. "Too? What do you mean?"

He shook his head. "Never mind. I just didn't want to lose you and was afraid that if you went off to war, I'd never see you again."

More silence, and Daddy cleared his throat, and I rose and folded the afghan. "I think I'll go lie down with Mama," I said.

He nodded, and I bent down awkwardly and hugged his shoulders. "Thanks, Daddy. Supper was delicious."

I lay beside Mama for a long time, my arm around her. Her breathing slowed, and her hand crept up and found mine. And eventually, we both fell asleep.

10

September 1945

Daddy and I, we developed sort of a routine over the next couple of months. We took turns caring for Mama and for ourselves, and after being home for a while, I stopped feeling so nervous around him.

We still didn't hug or talk a great deal, but we worked side by side and around the clock, and he even made beds while I scrubbed the floor, and all the while, Mama rocked.

He was right. You can't prescribe the will to live, and all we could do was keep on loving Mama and try not to feel angry. Angry at ourselves for whatever role we'd played in her shutting down, and angry at her for shutting down.

She wore the same clothes every day. It was one thing she insisted on, her washed-out daisy-print dress and the baggy green sweater. The sweater had been her mother's, Daddy told me. And he'd bought the daisy-print dress for her on their honeymoon.

So Daddy and I, we took turns scrubbing Mama's clothes at night while she slept and hanging them near the fireplace so they'd be warm and dry in the morning. And when I wasn't shopping for groceries or hanging up laundry or washing

Mama's face or cutting her nails or cooking supper, I was sleeping. But eventually I got caught up and began to feel restless.

I wasn't getting any younger, and the men returning from war were either engaged or shell-shocked or married with children, and everyone was focused on moving out of the city into nicer houses and getting nicer cars and bigger families, and here I was, dressing in dark print dresses most of the time because that's what spinsters were supposed to do—look dreadful and mournful. And how was one supposed to catch a man while looking dreadful?

Rosie the Riveter, the stereotype of women working in factories, had died. The war was over, and women were being called to reproduce, and I felt awfully useless. So I put on lipstick and did an up-do and went down to the hospital to speak with the head nurse about possible positions.

I wasn't about to sit around feeling sorry for myself. And I couldn't apply for a husband. So I'd apply for a job instead.

She reminded me of an army lieutenant, her back as straight as my daddy's ethics, and she was no-nonsense, and I liked this, after the war. I somehow missed the war, in a mournful, sadistic kind of way. I missed knowing I was needed. I missed fighting for something.

I felt a little lost, not having a clear, defined purpose, and Mama was normally the person I'd run to. She would have made me a cup of tea and told me it was going to be all right and calmed me down.

But all she did these days was rock and sleep, and try as he might, Daddy was no replacement for Mama.

They didn't need nurses, the head nurse told me. With the war over they'd let most of their nurses go, yet "there's about to be a baby boom," she said in her gruff voice, "so your best bet is midwifery."

I'd never been one to dream of having babies, really. I'd always been a career girl, a Virginia Woolf kind of woman, who longed for a room of her own. Maybe a husband too, but a room of her own. Nevertheless, I liked the idea of getting out of the house and getting a paycheck, so I said yes. I would become a midwife. And the head nurse took me down the hall to an office and introduced me to a short man with a protruding belly and a handlebar moustache.

His name was Dr. Archibald Kramer, he said. He was the obstetrician I'd be helping on home calls, the head nurse said. Then she turned and marched down the hall leaving Archibald and me to ourselves.

He was sitting at his desk eating a sandwich. It looked like bratwurst and pickles and he wiped at his mouth while standing, and his chair fell to the floor. "Good to meet you," he said, and his voice was as large as his middle. "Your name?"

"Um, it's Clara. Clara Anne Wilson. Good to meet you, Sir. Doctor."

He ahemed and cleared his throat for a minute, then said, "Pardon me, it's the bratwurst, you know. Hard to swallow. I'm Dr. Archibald, but you can just call me Archie."

I shook his extended hand.

"So what do you know of being a midwife?" he said, dusting crumbs from his jacket and pulling on wire-framed glasses.

"I was a nurse overseas in Normandy during the war," I said. "I attended Johns Hopkins and graduated with honors, and I'm hard-working and single, which frees me up considerably."

"I see. Have you ever assisted with a delivery?" he said, peering over his rims.

"Well, no," I said, scratching the back of my neck, "but I'm ready and eager to learn, if you'll just give me a chance, Sir. Doctor. Archie."

"Hmmm." Archie pulled out a large pocket watch. "Oh bother, these darn timepieces always stopping and here we go, then." He wound it. "Well, we need someone. And Hopkins is distinguished. Some fine crop they produce. Come on then, and we'll get you a uniform."

And he toddled off in his shiny oxfords, while I followed in my patent leathers.

⸻

It was October before I had my first house call, when the leaves were falling and everything was dying. I inhaled the scent of fallen leaves and fermenting apples and wondered why we were all so afraid of death when it smelled so inviting.

Daddy spoke of death at church that Sunday, and as of late his sermons had had an element of sorrow to them, and this made me strangely happy. Because I could finally relate to them.

And that was the day I first saw your grandfather. He had just returned from overseas, having fought against the Japanese, but he reminded me of Gareth somehow. There was a glint in his eye, and he sang in the pews with the voice of an angel, his tenor making me tremble, and we had such a small church it shook the rafters, too. But when he came up to introduce himself to Daddy after the service, Mama and I standing beside him as always, his voice was soft, and as he left, he walked with a limp. And he walked alone.

I thought about bringing him a pot of soup, but then Archie called and said there was a woman on Route 6 about to give birth; would I be able to assist him? And the soup would have to wait.

I packed Mattie's quilt. I wasn't sure why I did, but it was draped there over the wooden chair in my bedroom next to my dressing table, and I stared at it every morning as I brushed my hair and every evening as I massaged cold cream into my skin. So I folded it neatly and slid it into my satchel, pulled on the gray nursing scrubs Archie had given me, then packed some clean cloths, baby powder, olive oil, disinfectant, a sharp pair of scissors, and a couple of apples, should the delivery take hours.

Archie picked me up in his Rolls-Royce, and he was eating again, a hamburger, and there was mustard on his moustache.

It wouldn't always be this way, he said. Once I knew what I was doing, I'd need to find my own way of getting around. He would let me know the address, and I would go alone, and he'd be around in case of an emergency, but for now he'd show me the ropes.

It was about easing the mother into delivery and "You women tend to be better at those kinds of things than us men," he said, laughing, then wiping his moustache and clearing his throat.

I nodded politely and prayed the whole ride there, for I'd never been around babies. I was an only child, and because Daddy was a pastor, we lived far away from his family, and Mama had been an only child, too, so I was scared.

But I was more afraid of having nothing to do, of being stuck in a house with a mother who didn't know me, so I swallowed hard and stared out the car window. We were in the countryside, passing farms and fields and cows and then turning onto Route 6. All of a sudden, we were there in front of an old farmhouse with large curtainless windows and a sinking front porch and skinny cats that scattered when we approached.

Next to those cats, the farm seemed lifeless, with its sagging walls and everything just hanging on. And then a scream from inside the house jolted us into the house and down the hall and to the bedroom where a young woman lay white-faced in bed, the sheets all twisted and her hair a wet tangle.

"What took yous so long?" she said, but she was more terrified than angry, and in that moment I knew I could do this. I could calm her fears just as I had in Normandy, all those soldiers grasping wildly for kindness. So I dampened some cloths while Archie checked her pulse and felt her womb and asked about contractions. They were less than one minute apart and she screamed again, and I placed the cloths on her forehead and used the same voice I had with those soldiers.

"Shhhh, there, there, it's going to be all right," and I did this even as she screamed some more, and then I urged her to find something she could focus on, like the sky outside her window, to grip it like it was salvation when the contractions came. I'd learned this from Mama. This turning heavenward. Whenever life got too hard, she distracted herself with tea, but I'd always caught her staring at the sky while she waited for the kettle to sing.

Archie was washing his hands and humming all the while, and it bothered me a little. How can you hum when someone's life is in limbo? But I tried to stay focused on the girl who looked very young, maybe seventeen. Where her husband? Her mother? Anyone?

In between contractions she said her name was Jo, and she looked at me in a piercing way as if to ask me why she had to go through this. All I could do was squeeze her hand and say, "Remember the sky." She stared at it the whole time she pushed her baby boy out. And it was so much more than war;

it was the opposite of war, because her life was saved and one was created too. A miracle wrapped in mucus and blood and screaming at the top of his lungs.

She kept staring at the sky, even after Archie had cut the umbilical cord and he'd boiled the water and I cleaned up her son. "He's a fine-looking young man," said Archie. "Weighing a good seven pounds, and what a shock of hair!"

And she just kept looking out the window, until we'd wrapped the baby, who bellowed terrifically, in warm flannel and dabbed olive oil at the mucus in the corner of his eyes and pressed a cloth soaked in oil to his umbilical stump. Then we laid him on Jo's chest and she finally saw him. Saw her son for the first time, and love pulled him close to her, and he began to nurse immediately, and she touched his cheek with the most calloused of fingers.

It was then I saw the room, how bare it was, not even a dressing table, and just a thin blanket covering Jo, and those wide, blank windows. And I pulled the quilt Mattie had given me from my bag and wrapped it around the boy Jo had named Freddie.

And I said, "It's on loan. I'll collect it upon my return." Then I leaned in. "Well done, Jo. He's beautiful."

She looked at me as though I'd handed her the moon. She tucked the quilt tenderly around her nursing baby and said, "Thank you kindly." Like it had been way too long since someone had said anything nice to her.

We left then, Archie and I, Freddie and Jo asleep in bed, and I prayed God would be there with them, and I thanked him for being here, with me.

When I stepped from the Rolls-Royce to head up to the diner, Archie said, "You have a real knack, Clara." Then he drove off and my mouth went slack.

And I fairly skipped up the stairway—home.

11

I told Mama about little Freddie the next day after lunch, and we were both sitting in the living room, autumn leaves flying past the window like red and orange kites and for a moment, her eyes lit up. I think the greatest verse in the Bible is "Let there be light."

I told her about his chubby legs, about his eyes that pierced like his mama's and his shock of black hair. I told her about his yell, how it near split the universe in two, and I said, "You know, Mama? For the first time, I'm thinking about what it would be like to have kids and it kind of excites me," and she withdrew. Not physically, but her spirit just kind of fled, leaving her eyes vacant.

I sat there on the couch with my hands tucked between my knees wondering what I'd done, and she just hummed and rocked in her wooden chair.

"Tea, Mama?" I said, but she didn't seem to hear me. Just rocked and hummed and I took myself to my room and sat at my dressing table, looked in the mirror. Wondered who could ever love me.

Then Mama did the strangest thing—she came into my room and put her skinny arms around my shoulders.

And that was all.

She left soon after, went to lie down, and didn't rise again until supper. But I felt strong enough to walk a little straighter, and believe a little harder, that God could provide even me with a husband.

Three days later I biked to Jo's. It took me forty-five minutes, and I arrived panting and red-faced. Combines had harvested the fields, and hay bales dotted the landscape like the shredded wheat I'd had for breakfast.

The whole world seemed to be in perpetual celebration. Church bells rang somewhat continuously for all of the weddings, and everyone was up and moving. New automobiles were being constructed, and President Truman said we were the strongest, richest nation in the world.

And I could see America's biceps rippling across the fields until I arrived at Jo's collapsed farmyard.

She met me at the door with Freddie in her arms, wrapped in the quilt, his bright eyes peering out. "You look like a mother," I said to her, and she smiled. It made her pretty, the smile. Took the sallow yellow from her face and replaced it with a blush.

I set down my satchel and asked if I could have some water. It took her a while to find me a clean cup, but she did. It was smudged, and the water tasted like iron, but it was better than nothing.

"How do you feel?" I said, then.

"Oh, just flat tired 'tis all," said Jo. "Come in and seet a while?"

She pointed to the only couch in the house, next to an empty, despairing fireplace; but I said I should check Freddie out first.

It took a bit for his flailing arms and the way he squirmed, but his vitals and heart rate were good, and his weight was steady, and she said he was eating.

Then she took the quilt and folded it and thanked me for it, profusely, and I felt bad taking it back, only it was from Mattie.

"Jo, are you going to be okay?" I said then, sitting down on the couch and she, on an overstuffed chair. She began nursing and nodding.

"I think so. I mean, it ain't gonna be easy. But believe you me, it's better than if Freddie's daddy was here. He weren't a good man by any stretch."

She looked down at Freddie. "He left when I got pregnant, said he was finally enlisting; but I think he just got afeerd. He was a drunk, and I can't see him doing the army any good, and he knew he'd have to clean up his act for his boy."

I shook my head. "Up and leaving you like that, and you haven't heard anything from him?"

"No, and I don't right want to. My life is Freddie now. I'm gonna sell this place and move down South with my ma. I'm getting on welfare, and my ma, she's all alone, too, so she's gonna help me. At least, it's what she says now. Depends on whether or not she finds herself another feller before then."

I looked for a long moment at this young girl with her stringy mousy hair and her sallow skin, and I suddenly saw her for the glorious creature she was, fighting for her child. And I wondered if this was how all children saw us, in this beautiful, bright light.

I picked up the quilt and said, "Would you mind if I stitched Freddie's name in one of these squares? To remember him by? And perhaps to put a word beneath his name, like 'victorious' as sort of a blessing on his future?"

She began to cry then and held Freddie a little tighter. "It's the nicest thing anyone's ever done for me," she said then. "Thank you, ma'am. You're good people."

The bike ride home didn't seem long at all, thinking about Jo and how if she could be that strong, then I could too. My muscles ached when I arrived at the diner and climbed the stairs, but I gave Mama a big kiss.

Then I took out the quilt and lay it across her shoulders and said, "Mama, I'm going to use this quilt to bless babies."

I told her how I was going to stitch their names into the squares. There were sixty squares in total, blue and yellow, and each would be dedicated to a child, and beneath their names I'd put a word, a benediction of sorts, related to their story.

The blanket would be a gift to Mattie, honoring her dream to have a family with Gareth. I would give her a family, I told Mama, a family of children whose names were written in the stars—and in thread.

And Mama took the quilt into her arms, and she held it to her lips and kissed it, and then she rocked it as though it were a baby itself. And she sang it a lullaby and I left her alone for a while, and afterward, she rose from the chair and went into the kitchen and did something she hadn't done in years. She cooked Daddy and me supper.

After Mama's feast of fried yams and herb chicken and mashed potatoes, Daddy and I cleaned up while Mama went to bed, exhausted from her efforts. And Daddy and I, we just worked side by side, not saying much, both contemplating what had happened. Mama had used too many dishes and ingredients were scattered across the kitchen, but every once in a while we smiled, for the miracle in it all.

"Daddy," I said, scrubbing chicken grease from a pan, late October skies streaming primrose across our windows. "Just wondering whether, well, you and Mama had ever thought of having more children?"

Daddy nearly dropped the plate he was holding, and then he set it down gently on the counter and looked at me. Scratching his balding head, he said, "Why do you ask?"

I shook my head and handed him the pan. "No reason, really. It's just, well . . . when I told Mama about my day with Jo and her baby, and then said how I was going to stitch Freddie's name in the blanket, she acted kind of strange. It was the first time in a long time I've seen her happy, and I just wondered if, well, you know . . . if she'd ever wanted a bigger family."

Daddy sighed, rubbed his eyes. "Maybe it's time you and I had some tea."

I drained the dishwater, turned on the kettle, and cut some lemon loaf while Daddy finished putting away the dishes. Then we sat at the table, and Daddy cleared his throat and wrapped his fingers around his cup.

"You weren't our only child," he said.

And I sat still. "What do you mean?"

Daddy looked across the room, and I followed his gaze to the photo frames on the mantle. "I mean, your mother had seven children. But six of them died either by miscarriage or prematurely, and we had to dig so many tiny graves . . ." His voice broke, and he sipped some tea, and I just stared at him.

"We'd actually given up hope of having any children at all, and your mother, she just couldn't take it anymore. It's when she started taking her nerve medicine. And then . . . you came along."

I'd never seen my daddy cry and it was worse than almost anything I'd seen on the front lines. He looked at me with red eyes. I swallowed.

"And we could hardly believe it," said Daddy. "You were the strongest little kid." He laughed a little, in a choking kind of way. "You wouldn't even let us put your diaper on, you were always squirming out of reach and thought it was a big game, and by the time you were two and a half, you insisted on dressing yourself. 'I do it,' you used to say."

I thought of Freddie, flailing and bright-eyed, and Daddy stood now in the fading light, walked to the kitchen window. In the far room, Mama lay beneath piles of afghans, and I thought of her thin body, excavated of life, and how she'd never said anything, all these years.

"Your mama was so afraid of losing you. She barely let you out of her sight. Things like your first step, your first bike ride, your first swim in the ocean—these were really painful for her because they all symbolized you being taken from her.

"And I was afraid, too, of losing you and of what it might do to your mama. Part of me, I guess, didn't let myself get close to you for fear you would die, too." His profile was grave, and as he looked at me, he was the epitome of sorrow. "I'm so sorry, Clara. I wish I could take back all of those years and do them over."

I nodded but couldn't speak. He glanced toward the window and shoved his hands into his pockets. "And then you said you were going to join the army . . ."

I hated myself. I put my head in my hands and shook for the realization. Mama hadn't been mad at Daddy. Daddy had been trying to protect his family. They'd both been afraid of losing me.

"And I tried, I tried to get you to stay, but you're so stubborn, girl," and Daddy looked at me and laughed a little. "I guess you get that from me. And in any normal circumstance, it wouldn't have been so bad, but . . . well, your mama she just kind of shut down afterward. I guess it was the last straw. She was just convinced she'd lost you forever."

I stood then and went to Daddy and said, "I'm so sorry," in a voice very much not my own, and he pulled me close then, something he'd never really done before, and he smelled like shaving soap.

"You didn't know," he said, and we both stood there for a long time, watching the world turn dark. And stars, thousands of tiny emblems of light, all over the place.

Mama was stirring in bed, and I went in and lay down beside her, saying softly, "Seven babies, Mama." She opened her eyes and looked at me.

And I saw all of those funerals, all of those good-byes, all of those pregnancies, and the washing of blood and the buried dreams. She'd hidden it for so many years, but she was too weak now to hide anything.

"My brothers and sisters," I said, and she began to cry then. She sobbed as I held her. And I whispered prayers into her hair and asked God to have mercy.

Eventually we rose, our clothes rumpled, our faces swollen, and we splashed cold water on them. I sat down with my needle and thread while Mama made herself some tea. I stitched Freddie's name in cursive, delicate white thread across one of the blue squares. Beneath it, I wrote "victorious."

It was late by the time I finished, and Daddy was reading on the couch, one of his theology texts, and Mama was snoozing in her chair, and I placed the quilt in her arms.

"Mama," I said, and her eyelids fluttered open. "Will you take care of these children for me?"

And she held the quilt close to her heart and traced Freddie's name and rocked him long into the night. And come morning we found her asleep with the quilt cradled in her arms, and for the first time in a long time, there was a smile on her lips.

12

Snow fell at Christmas on trees, on bushes, on rooftops like Flynn's vanilla malt all droopy and white. Flynn grew Christmas trees, and Mama and I bought one and put it in our living room. We decorated it with pipe-cleaner ornaments and shiny balls and popcorn. Carols played on the radio that daddy had inherited from his papa and mama, and I hummed along, while Daddy made a fire in the fireplace.

It was as though baby Jesus was being born this very year, everyone pulling out all the stops, including Daddy with his live Nativity. After all, he said, his girl was home from war, and there was much to rejoice in. And I figured it's how most everybody felt. It was a season for rejoicing. Peacetime was prosperous, and the world was slowly healing from Nazism.

Oliver Flanagan, the shy soldier with the limp, built a manger to lay baby Jesus in for the Nativity. I'd seen him every Sunday since arriving home, and he would just slip out the doors at the end of service. And every time he walked away, I felt a deep sense of loss. Was it compassion? Or did I miss a man I didn't even know?

Come Christmas, Mama had improved drastically with the arrival of each new baby. Sometimes on her sad nights, she still rocked the quilt to sleep, but more often than not these days she could be seen laughing. And she invited all of the lonely and forgotten over for a free meal, as she used to do before the war, using the diner—which was closed Christmas Day—to seat them.

And this year, Oliver was among those who came, and I had my red curls done up for the festive season and my apron on, looking very much like the homemaker I wasn't.

It would be the first time we'd talk to each other.

I brought him a plate of turkey and stuffing and mashed potatoes with gravy and asked if he would like tea or coffee.

"Um," he said, lowering his eyes a bit and he had a strong nose, I thought, and cheekbones, too. His face was long, as were his fingers, and he had thick blond hair that hung over his left eye. "I, well, what would you suggest?"

I smiled, setting down his plate. "I hear the coffee's pretty good. But I'm a tea girl myself."

He played with his napkin. "Tea sounds great. Thank you."

I'd never been so careful making tea, and as I brought it to him, it wobbled and spilt on my white apron. Oliver jumped to his feet and grabbed a napkin, said, "I'm so sorry," as he tried to clean me up, and everyone was looking at us then.

"I'm a clumsy girl," I said, handing him the cup and rushing to the back of the diner to sit in a bathroom stall and wonder at how I fumbled everything up, and why was I so nervous around this man?

After I'd breathed in and out and pinched my cheeks, I returned to serving tables, purposely avoiding his, and Mama took over, not asking why. At the end of the night she handed me a napkin, with a note in beautiful scrawl that said, "Thank you for the wonderful tea. Merry Christmas. Oliver."

I'm not ashamed to say I held onto the napkin for months. Not knowing why, I did my hair extra special every Sunday after that.

But then there was Sandra. She was pregnant when she received a telegram at the end of the war, the kind of telegram that leaves you gripping the walls, the doors, anything to keep you standing after your heart has died.

And there were Glenda and Helen, whose husbands had been drafted to fight Japan near the end of the battle, prisoners of war, tortured in their cells and returned home alcoholics. The torture continued, even after the United Nations was formed in October 1945, but it didn't seem to matter to them. Because they were stuck in the past. And I wondered if it was better to know your husband was dead than for him to be perpetually dying.

And I was the one to deliver their babies that winter. Stitching their children's names into the cloth of the quilt while their mothers wept.

And I saw it in their eyes when they looked at their sons or daughters who resembled their fathers: pride and immense sorrow and the fear of raising a child alone. I decided I didn't need to marry. Ever. It was too painful, the thought of possibly losing someone, and what if he stopped loving you?

So I stopped pinning my hair nicely on Sundays, and I pretended to stop noticing the bouquets of flowers someone kept leaving by our door in the early spring, with the scrawled handwriting. And I tried hard not to think about how long Oliver must have taken to carve the jewelry box for my birthday in May, and how did he know it was my birthday?

Men weren't supposed to give single women gifts. I knew this, and I expected Daddy to say something when he found them in my room, but instead he picked up the box, his fingers tracing the delicate carving, and said, "What beautiful workmanship."

And I kept it all. Exchanging old bouquets for new ones in the vase by my window, and putting the jewelry box by my bed although I owned no jewelry because Daddy thought it was frivolous.

It was the bicycle that made me angry.

For so long now, I'd been riding my bike on its metal rims, and thankfully Daddy had driven me to the home births all winter. Come springtime, though, I biked sometimes to exercise, my tires deflated and cracked over winter. I'd wrapped wool around them like they used to do in wartime, and it made for a softer ride. I kept telling myself to just go and buy new tires, but I was trying to save my money because now that I'd decided not to marry I needed to support myself.

And then one morning in June when the poppies were blooming and lemonade stands were popping up around the block, I walked down the stairs to go to work and there sat a brand-new bike, with my name in doggone cursive on a note on the seat and a red bow around the handlebars. It was shiny and new and beautiful, and I got so angry I just turned around and stomped upstairs in a quiet fume.

I sat on my couch and got my uniform all wrinkly, and then I stomped around some more, Mama just watching and eventually she rose from her knitting, put a hand on my shoulder, and said, "Clara, what's wrong?"

I exploded. "Darn Oliver Flanagan. He got me a bike. He's just making it so hard."

Mama was silent for a moment, and then she began to laugh. I'd never seen her laugh so hard. She even put a hand on her waist and said, "Oh dear, it hurts," and then kept on.

Eventually, she realized I wasn't laughing, not even in the slightest, and she wiped the tears from her eyes. "I'm sorry, honey," she said. "It's just . . . well . . . he's making it so hard to what? To not like him?"

I sat down with a thud and burst into tears, and she sat down, too. "I'm a silly old woman. Don't pay me any mind . . ."

I shook my head, and my face was burning. "Mama, I just don't want to get married because it will hurt too much. Losing him, someday, it will hurt and I don't think I can go through it. I mean, look at you and all the loss you've gone through, and you're so much stronger than me."

Again, Mama was quiet, and she held me for a while and then said softly, "Yes, it's true I guess. But Clara, you'll never get to go through the joy of having them in the first place. I mean, if I hadn't gone through the loss of six babies, I would never have had you, now would I?"

I knew I would be late for Mrs. Thompson's delivery so I dried my eyes on Mama's handkerchief and kissed her cheek. "Thank you, Mama. I love you."

And I left knowing Mama was sitting there, praying for her only daughter. And I left confident in this love.

In spite of my confidence in Mama, I rode the shiny new bike right over to your grandfather's after delivering Mrs. Thompson's daughter, and I rode it good and hard with the wind tearing at my curls like it was trying to hold me back.

But nothing can hold back a redhead, so I arrived, flushed from the sun and looking quite a sight, I am sure.

I stomped up to Oliver's front steps and knocked at his door and no one answered. And I pursed my lips and knocked again and then walked around the house, his blue Chevy parked out front, the same truck he drove to church each Sunday.

His house was small and solid and set in stone, and ivy climbed the walls. The yard had wooden benches with intricate carving, and there was a trellis as I rounded the stone wall, and roses. And in place of a vegetable garden, flowers, a triangular plot of them: Jacob's ladder, coneflowers, asters, petunias, irises, sunflowers, daisies, and poppies—pink, purple, yellow—columbine and hollyhocks, tall and gangly. And there he was, bent in the middle of it all, weeding and singing. And who can be angry in the face of such beauty?

I recognized my bouquets from his flowers. I saw the tender way he turned the soil, the way his head tilted as though listening to the blooms even as he sang, and I turned on my dusty soles to leave.

"Clara?" His voice, behind me. "Is it you?"

I felt like crying.

"Yes," I said, turning.

"Smell this." He walked toward me in his overalls, a cluster of green in his hands, and put something in my palm, and I held it to my nose.

"It's like a peppermint candy," I said.

He smiled shyly. "Mint," he said. "Isn't it wonderful?"

I nodded.

"Can I . . . won't you . . . do you want some tea?" he said.

And I dug deep for the resolve that had pedaled me here.

"Listen, Oliver," I said, and he listened. His whole face listened, as it had to the flowers. "Thank you for sending me bouquets and beautiful things like the jewelry box and the bike," and he looked down, the tips of his ears pink.

"And you seem like a very nice man and I'm honored, truly," and he looked up, then, "but I'm afraid . . . ," and here I paused, "I'm not able to pursue a relationship with you."

He didn't say anything.

"I . . . well . . . I hope I haven't misunderstood your intentions," I said then, searching him, "but I didn't want you to keep wasting such beautiful gifts on me."

Oliver nodded, a slow, graceful motion. "I understand. But I'd still like to make you some tea."

So we sat at his wooden table in a quiet kitchen with herbs on the sill and the kettle whistling, and I looked around at the way this man lived. At the bookshelves lining the living room walls, at the record player and a piano in the corner and a guitar in another.

A radio in the kitchen played Strauss, and Oliver put sprigs of mint in the tea and set it down before me. I sipped as he asked me if I read books and said I was welcome to borrow from his library.

So after our mugs, I stood and browsed and found poetry by Wordsworth and theology by Charles Spurgeon, romance by Charlotte Brontë, and theories by Einstein.

Then I handed the books back to him and shook my head and sat down on his settee. He sat beside me, and I said, "I really must go."

"Your books?" he said, holding them out, and I shook my head.

"I just can't take anything more from you. It would be wrong."

He nodded, and I walked to the door, and he held it open as I left.

"Good-bye," I said, turning at the end of the walkway.

"Good-bye."

Then, "Clara?" I turned, a little. "I'll be here, if you need me."

And I said nothing, just kept walking, leaving the bike behind, the sun setting the way it always does.

13

Oliver pulled back the sheets to climb in, and Clara was tucked inside in her cotton nightgown, her white hair up in curlers. She'd never intended to be the kind of person who wore curlers, but there they were, and here she was.

Funny, she thought, how she was all of the ages she'd ever been—the young, impulsive girl who just graduated nursing school; the new army recruit on the boat with Eva; the insomniac in the tent bowing low in the dirt of France; and the woman wrapping babies in Mattie's quilt—and she was all of these ages, in this wrinkled old body. Kind of like an egg roll or something, and she laughed a little to herself and Oliver smiling at her.

It took some time for Oliver to ease into bed, but eventually he was lying beside her. "I love you, Mister Flanagan," she said then, reaching out a hand she no longer recognized, a hand with a ring he'd designed himself, of a trumpet lily opening up to a diamond, its stem wrapped around her finger.

He took her hand and said, "I love you, too, Mrs. Flanagan."

His gray hair still hung over his eye, and his hands were still knotted and strong from woodwork he could no longer do.

Yet he whittled. And he never complained. Once you come close to death, he said, life—just the very fact of it—turns into a gift.

They lay there for a while in the dark in the hotel in Knoxville, Tennessee. It had been a long drive today, another six and a half hours after lunch and Clara telling her story to an eager audience, and she hadn't talked this much in what felt like years.

Back home, in their little stone house, she and Oliver mostly played music and cards and read books.

But tonight she wanted to hear him speak, more than anything. Because she suddenly missed him with an ache, as though telling stories about the past had hung some curtain between them, and she tore at this curtain with, "Why do you love me, Oliver?"

He looked at her across the white sheets for a while, and then he said, "Because, Clara, I need you."

And to some extent she knew this, for his body depended on assistance: climbing out of bed, shaving, feeding, it all required her help.

"Do you mean, you need me to be your cook and maid?" she said, half-teasing but her eyebrows raised.

He said, "Come close to me," so she slid over and the curtain fell.

Then he took her hand, and they gripped each other in the darkness. "I knew I needed you the first Sunday I saw you, sitting with your mama in your daddy's church." He was quiet for some time, then, "Your whole face was lit up like an angel's and your hair, it was fire-red, and everything about you glowed something fierce."

Clara laughed a little. "Weren't you scared of getting burned?"

He squeezed her hand. "No, I was too cold to be afraid of fire. You were the most beautiful person I'd ever seen, and it was as though my whole heart leapt out of my chest and into your hands."

Clara sighed. "And then I crushed it."

"No . . . no, more like, suffocated it."

She traced his lips. "I need you, too. Desperately."

He turned then, a tedious feat for him, and he wrapped his long arms around her. "I know you do," he said.

Long after Oliver had fallen asleep, a gentle snoring in her ear and Knoxville traffic outside their hotel window, she thought of the caravan they'd made, the caravan of family and how each person in each of those cars was unique, like a square in a quilt and together they made a blanket. And she hoped this for her family, to be a covering for the wounded and the hurting, to be the kind of quilt that had healed Mama, God rest her soul.

Mama had been strong until the end. She'd been the one to plan Daddy's funeral when he passed away from a heart attack, and she'd stood up front and sung "The Lord Is My Shepherd" in the sweet soprano.

It had been twenty years since Mama had passed away, but even there in the circle of Oliver's arms Clara suddenly felt hollowed out. And she wondered if Mama and Daddy were still married in heaven; she knew the Bible said they wouldn't be, but how else would she recognize them?

And she began to cry at the thought of not being married to Oliver in heaven, and he kissed her neck in his sleep. "What's wrong?" His voice was a whisper.

"Don't leave me," she said then as she had back in 1960 when he'd lost his hand.

"I can't," he said then, waking. "We're one person. If I go, you go."

They rose early the next morning. It was Wednesday. They were meeting up with Mattie on Friday and still had nine hours of driving.

The family piled in, and Noah was up front now, Shane beside Clara who preferred the back because when she talked, she could see her listeners.

She was wearing one of Mama's sweaters today, a purple one that reminded her of the lilac bush, and it was something that had changed, too. The bush and the diner were gone, her childhood home, gone, replaced by a Mini Mart, and she dabbed at her eyes with the edge of the sweater and it felt good to be close to her mother.

And there were nights when she'd pull out her father's old leather Bible, all cracked and worn, and she'd blot the pages with tears for the underlining of verses and the notes in the margins and the way he'd pored over Scripture every morning before breakfast.

She'd done so this morning, over coffee and eggs in the hotel lounge, all of her family gathered as though she were dying, and she'd read to them from Psalm 68. They'd all listened in silence, even tiny Elise, to Grandma reading from Great-Granddaddy's Bible.

> Sing unto God, sing praises to his name: extol
> him that rideth upon the heavens by his name
> JĀH, and rejoice before him.
> A father of the fatherless, and a judge of the
> widows, is God in his holy habitation.

God setteth the solitary in families: he bringeth
out those which are bound with chains: but the
rebellious dwell in a dry land.

"God setteth the solitary in families." she said now, patting
Shane's arm. He had always been such a gentle boy. Even the
way he folded his hands in his lap, as though he were praying.
And she put her hands on his, and he said, "Hi, Mom."

She smiled up at him. "Hi, son."

It hadn't taken long to become a mother, but how it had
thrown her. To nurture a life whose features were those of a
woman she'd watched die just hours earlier. And Clara wondered again, even as Noah turned on a band called Matchbox
Twenty and Oliver shook his head at the rock and roll, she
wondered why God had chosen her.

They pulled out onto U.S. Route 411, Oliver insisting on
continuing to drive, for it was one thing he could still do, one
way in which he could serve them.

The month of May was full-swing in the fields along the
highway—in the shoots of corn and wide-leafed soybeans and
the white-cloud cotton. Clara leaned her head against the seat
and thought maybe she'd rest awhile. She was seventy-seven
years old, and her body was tired. She kept one hand on
Shane's. The music was catchy, and she was beginning to doze
when, "Grandma, I've got this girl, and I was wondering if you
could give me some advice?"

Clara opened her eyes and found Noah and his hayfield
hair, his freckled skin, turned around in the front seat and he
was too little to care about girls. But then she blinked and he
was older now, and she laughed and said, "What does an old
woman like me know about you young whippersnappers?"

Noah laughed, too, and he was a lovely boy, she thought.
The way he threw back his head and the shine in his eyes.

"Okay, okay," she said then. "Tell me about this girl."

"All right, well, her name is Samantha, and well, I like her. And, um, I'm not sure what to do."

Clara glanced over at Shane who was watching her, and she knew he knew about Samantha. He was the kind of father who took his son to baseball games and who led Boy Scouts and who tucked his kids in every night. The kind of father Oliver had been, and she said, "Well, it's a start. She has a name. Now, does she know you exist?"

Noah hung his head. "No," he said, then looked at her eagerly. Oliver glanced over, chuckling. "That's why I need your help."

"Oh dear," Clara said. "Well, let's see. Are you in any of the same classes?"

"No."

"Well, tell me, dear boy, what is it you like about this girl? And how do you know her?"

Outside there were cows grazing, and the world was pastoral as Oliver turned down the music and Noah told them of Samantha's brown eyes and the way she stood in the cafeteria line and the song she'd sung at the school musical and how she was a year older than him.

"You're smitten, that much is clear," Clara said when it was over, and Shane said in a whisper, "You have no idea."

"Dad!" Noah reached across the seat and pretended to punch Shane in the arm.

"Well, honey," said Clara, "I'm not sure how much help I can be. I didn't date a lot, back in the day. There was Henry, and then your grandpa here, and our dating life, well, it was . . ." Oliver glanced at her in the rearview, "short, and rather unremarkable, wouldn't you say, honey?"

Oliver shook his head. He spoke slowly. "It was anything but unremarkable," he said. "It was short, yes, but we'd known each other for years. And it was very remarkable. Because God was in it. All of it."

Clara nodded, "That's right, Oliver. You're right, as always, and, Noah, I should have asked this first, but is this girl a believer? Because Noah," and here, she pulled her hand from Shane's and placed it on the boy's shoulder in front of her, "without God there is nothing good. So without him, I have no advice."

Noah sighed. "I know, Grandma." He looked at his father who nodded slightly. "I really don't know if she believes in God. I don't know anything except she's pretty and she's a good singer and I think about her all the time."

Clara smiled. "It's okay, honey. You're allowed to have crushes. Just don't go and marry the girl right yet . . ."

Noah turned, and for a while the world was the beat of a teenager's music and the rough of the wheel against asphalt. And then, Noah looked back. "Can you still tell me how you and Grandpa ended up getting married, Grandma? I mean, maybe it will give me some ideas or something."

Clara straightened up. "Very well, then. But keep in mind, it's a story about God, Noah. About the way he loved your Daddy so much he put two old people like us together to give him a family, and that is what God does, Noah. He sets the lonely in families."

14

Summer 1950

Boys scared me and intrigued me, and I never quite knew what to do with them.

Even when Henry took me for the malt, back when I was sixteen, I played around with the straw and swivelled on my stool and talked too much. And when he kissed me I laughed a little. It probably had to do with my relationship with Daddy. Or maybe I was just a clumsy, awkward girl.

We eventually learned to love each other, though—Daddy and me—after I came home from the war. We became friends when Mama stopped talking and we realized how much we were alike—Daddy spending the evenings reading the Bible and me, the paper, and Mama rocking, and the whole house a symposium of quiet.

Anything I did know about boys I learned from Eva, who knew way too much, and I'll never forget the day she moved back to Smithers after the war. She might as well have been wearing a torn veil for all the heartache on her face, the wedding ring still on her finger and her moving in with her parents and getting a job waitressing at the diner.

And we tried to be friends. She told me about Luc, the French soldier, whom she'd run away with to his home village of Oradour-sur-Glane, how they'd met his family and then gone to the Catholic church.

The priest had married them, and even as the church bells had rung—her in an ivory dress borrowed from his mother and him in his uniform—shots had rung out and a bomb had gone off fifty meters away. The priest had fled, the wedding was over, and the town was up in smoke. And they were lucky to have hidden in the rafters of the church, because 642 townspeople were killed by the German Waffen-SS company.

And when Luc's family learned their house had burned down, they did their Hail Marys and cursed the demons of war and lit a thousand candles when the company had fled the town, a pile of rubble and ashes and corpses.

Then the family turned on Eva, saying she'd been the omen, she'd brought bad luck to the town, and Luc, with his mama's arm around his waist, said nothing, just bore a sudden resemblance to her, and Eva ripped off the ivory dress and ran in her slip, far, far from the church through the smoke, into the woods and hoping all the while Luc would chase her.

And he didn't.

So Eva had found work on a farm, having given her army wages to Luc and too ashamed to wire home for money. She'd pretended she was married, she was fine, and her parents had no idea Eva was milking cows and collecting eggs and weeding the garden for an old French couple who fed her scraps and gave her a barn loft to sleep in. And eventually she earned enough money to take the train to Marseille and the ship to New York, followed by another train ride home. All skinny and bedraggled-looking.

"I'm still in love with him, Clara," she said.

Eva had worked for five years on that French farm, and not once had Luc tried to contact her.

I hugged Eva, said I had to go to work. But really, I just had to go. To process all of this—her needing a man who wasn't available. And her needing me suddenly, in his place. And even though it hurt, I took her banana bread that night, to her room in her parents' mansion where she sat curling her hair, and we ate the bread on her bed and laughed about me having set the army tent on fire and her running off with a Frenchman.

Because life is short, Noah. So we need to make amends.

But then after a few months of meeting after work and talking about the war we realized we didn't have much else to talk about. Then Eva found a new friend, a girl named Sally who was also a waitress at the diner and dating a boy named Edward. Sally hooked Eva up with a guy named Fred, and they double-dated while I stayed at home and read the paper.

Those were lonely years. I had been rejected twice by Eva, and I spent a lot of time trying to figure out what was wrong with me.

Most girls were getting married or having babies, and every Sunday I saw your grandpa at church. Every Sunday he tipped his hat at me and I felt something akin to compassion or love, I wasn't sure, and he would have made a nice friend, I thought.

But we were taught men and women couldn't be friends, just spouses or nothing. And it didn't seem fair to me.

There were no more flowers, no more shiny bikes, no more carved gifts, just Oliver's unassuming limp out of the church to his truck each Sunday.

Mama would look at me mournfully every time he passed; then when we'd get home she'd make a pot of tea and not drink it, just stare out the window, the kettle whistling until it ran dry, and one day she found me in my bedroom packing my old satchel and a leather suitcase I'd bought from Macy's on a shopping trip to Baltimore.

"Hi, Clara," she said, stepping into the room, her arms folded across her chest. She wore a cardigan, even though the air was humid, and a dress I had bought her for her birthday in February—sage green with brown paisley. Her red hair was up in its loose bun. "Where are you going?"

I looked down at the quilt, the one with the babies' names stitched across, five years of deliveries; and beneath every name, a promise in threaded cursive: "saved" or "cherished" or "beautiful," and the year, too. It had become a tapestry, a timeline of hope, and Mama reached out and I hugged her shoulders.

"It's time, Mama," I said then, and she gripped the quilt close as though it could save her. "I'm moving down the street into Mrs. Bailey's place. She provides room and board, and it's high time I accepted I'm single, Mama. I need to find my own way now," I said, stuffing socks and nylons and panties into the mesh bag of the case. "I can't depend on you and Daddy forever."

"But you can!" she said then, a quiet desperation in her eyes.

I stopped and looked at my dear mama, and I put my hands on her shoulders and said, "You're not gonna lose me. I'll still be here. Just not in the same house, but I'm not leaving you, okay? I'll visit you all the time, but I need my own space, you know?"

And she surprised me then, folded the quilt, tucked it into the suitcase beside my piles of skirts and blouses, and said, "You're absolutely right, Clara. This is good. It's hard, but it's good and, just a minute, please."

She began to cry but visibly pulled herself together, like stretching out a crumpled piece of tissue, and she said, "Now, how can I help you?"

I hugged her tight. "I'm scared, Mama," I said, like I was five years old again.

"It will be okay," she said. "You will do just fine."

And we packed the rest of my wardrobe into those two pieces of luggage, and then we sat and drank tea like old times, the radio on in the background, my coat on and my bags at the door.

Mrs. Bailey's room was small and cozy and perfect, I told myself over and over as I sat on my bed and folded my knees to my chest and held myself like my mama used to do, to ease the pain knifing my heart. If only I could just belong somewhere. I felt like a nuisance to everyone and to no one, and as much as I was afraid of being hurt in a relationship, I wondered if loneliness didn't hurt more.

Holding myself helped a bit, and after a while I felt strong enough to stand, even as the sun peered through my window; and though my parents lived down the street, they felt as far as they had when I was overseas.

Lace curtains dangled from my windows, and it really was a lovely room. I hung the baby quilt over the pink sitting chair in the corner, and an oak dresser soon held my clothes. The oval mirror above the dresser revealed a very sad girl, and I splashed water on her cheeks, brushed her hair with gentleness, and spoke kindly to her reflection. "You are brave," I told her. "You are strong and able, and God is with you and you can do this."

It was six-thirty, according to my wristwatch, the silver one Eva had given me so long ago when we were still friends, before the war, before everything changed. Funny how time keeps on ticking even as friendships and events and hearts come to a standstill.

Six-thirty was suppertime, Mrs. Bailey had said, the plump woman in the frilled apron who'd answered the door with flour on her hands. She was boisterous and forgetful and laughed a lot, and she'd lost her husband in the First War.

The money from renting out the upstairs room, the guest room, would help tremendously, she said. And this made me feel better about my decision until the door closed behind me and I stood alone. Four strange walls staring me down.

I headed down the winding staircase, black-and-white photographs lining the way, and at the bottom, a fox terrier licked my hands. The place smelled of rosemary and chicken, and Mrs. Bailey called, "Yoo-hoo, Clara? Suppertime, dear!" and it suddenly felt a bit like home.

We talked late into the night around the dinner table, the chicken dish followed by biscuits with strawberry jam followed by steaming tea and a cuckoo clock calling out the hours and a candle flickering in the window.

Mrs. Bailey learned of my serving in Normandy and pulled out her handkerchief as she talked about Charlie, who'd enlisted during World War I at age thirty-five when they had four little ones at home. He'd died and she'd raised her babies alone.

"All four of them," she said, sniffing and clucking and dabbing at her eyes with the edge of her apron. "How he loved his babies, but he loved his country more. Poor silly man, poor noble man," and she smoothed out her apron, and then she pulled out her photo album. "Charlie was handsome," I said.

And then a photo in which he had his arms around his children, and Mrs. Bailey smiled. "He would balance them all on his knees and read *Tom Sawyer* and *Huckleberry Finn*, and they'd all just nestle their sweet little heads against him and oh, my, look at me, carrying on so. More tea, dear?"

Without waiting for me to answer she stood and bustled around filling a plate with cookies and topping up my mug with tea and starting the dishes.

Then she sat back down, said, "Now where was I? Oh yes. I was going to ask you about you. So tell me, dear . . . do you have a beau?"

I stirred my tea longer than necessary. "No," I said finally, "I don't. I turned down the one person interested, and now I'm afraid I'll be alone forever."

Mrs. Bailey clucked again. "Nonsense, not a pretty thing like yourself. We'll find you someone, don't you worry, dear. Just give me time. I know every good-looking lad from here to Baltimore city, and I know they'll be lining up at the gate to marry a beautiful redhead like yourself."

I laughed. "You're too kind, but see, I don't really want to get married."

Mrs. Bailey set her teacup down and said, "Sorry, dear?"

"I don't want to get married. I mean, I do, but I don't want to lose someone, you know, or get hurt, so I have chosen not to get married."

Mrs. Bailey rose again and cleared some dishes and me thinking I'd maybe hurt her feelings and the candle flickering madly.

I was preparing an apology when she sat down and put her hand on mine and said, "You know, honey, I get it. I do. It hurts like the dickens. But in spite of Charlie dying and me raising four babies on my own, there hasn't been a day in which I've regretted marrying him. Not one blessed day. Because those years we had together were wonderful, and they gave us children, who are the light of my life."

She paused there, and I waited because I wanted more. Her words tasted like hope, and I was ravenous.

Mrs. Bailey sat back in her chair. "I don't know, honey. I don't want to tell you what to do. But sometimes, the only way we can know love is to know pain. Because the pain makes the love so special, you know?"

I thought about it. I thought about Gareth's letter to Mattie, about him singing "Amazing Grace" while dying. "It's kind of like faith," I said. "The greater the risk, the greater the faith."

Mrs. Bailey nodded. "You're so right, my girl! I think this calls for some chocolate."

She pulled chocolate truffles from her pantry, and they tasted like heaven. I wondered if love did, too.

15

November 1950

Everything changed the day I met Nancy Kirkpatrick.

It was November 11, 1950. Remembrance Day. A day I would always remember, and it was fall, a cold fall, in which the trees barely had a chance to turn color before the wind wiped them clean. I'd gotten a call saying Nancy was having her baby, and would I come? I'd learned to drive by this point and took my 1940 Plymouth, which I'd bought with Daddy's help from a used car salesman for just twenty-five dollars, to a farm in the fields of nowhere.

The house was swallowed up by a hovering sky. Sheep bleated when I stepped from the car, and I ran to the door, but no one answered. When I stepped into the house, I saw blood pooling its way from the kitchen to the living room across the carpet and to the couch where Nancy lay giving birth all by herself on an old tablecloth she must have snagged on the way.

I couldn't get there fast enough to take a pulse that was fluttering, and her eyes were holding up the ceiling, just riveted, and her knuckles were white as she gripped my hands, but she said nothing. Just clenched her teeth and bore holes into the tiles and pushed. I needed to call Archie. This was an emergency, but I couldn't leave her and yet she was dying.

I felt powerless, but even in those moments she pushed with everything in her, and I could see her heart failing. She was such a tiny lady and her body, just kind of turning inside-out in a huge way for this child.

So I wiped her forehead with a clean cloth and urged her to push and breathe and push, honey, push there darlin', because it was obvious she wanted nothing more than to produce life. The baby's head was crowning, even as Nancy's heart was failing.

I have never tried to help a baby exit the way I helped him, in the hopes I might ease some of the pressure, but her face was so white it was no use. And even as Nancy's son split the air with the sound of his lungs expanding, she whispered, "Take good care of him for me?"

And her death reminded me of the crucifixion, the unfairness in it all, the sacrifice.

───❀───

Archie got there as fast as his Rolls-Royce could on gravel, but the ambulance beat him. Nancy was on the stretcher, but she'd already gone, they said. Her heart, given out so her child's could give way, and the baby boy stretched and pulled and yawned in my arms and I held him close while he whimpered. I wrapped him in flannel and then the quilt, and he was rooting. So I placed him against his mother's chest before they wheeled her away, and I let him nurse, Nancy's arms limp at her side.

Then they took her away, and Archie and I sat at Nancy's kitchen table, the floor wiped clean and her child asleep in my arms, as we scanned her papers and I mostly sat shocked.

Staring down at a head of brown hair and the fullest cheeks I'd ever seen and his little fingers working even as he slept.

Part of me loved him so desperately, and part of me felt something close to loathing for the way he'd robbed his mother of life. Yet she had given it so willingly and would have done it again, this woman whose husband had died of cancer just months earlier.

But here he was, the little boy she'd bore and the most handsome of newborns I'd ever laid eyes on, and she'd asked me to take care of him.

"Well, then, you'd better darn well take care of him," Archie said, rolling a cigar as he left, the papers in his hands. "When the dying ask, you give," and saying so, he took off in his Rolls, leaving me alone with a baby in my arms.

I drove him home tucked in blankets in a cardboard box in the backseat of my Plymouth, and Mama came over right away and spent the next few nights with me. Mrs. Bailey was a constant presence, too, hauling down bags of old baby clothes from her attic. We hired a wet nurse to feed him during the day, and at night, we used a bottle.

Those first few days, I just sat on my bed while Mama held him and sang to him. I sat there feeling as shell-shocked as the day I came home from Normandy, wondering what life had thrown me and how I could ever be a mother.

"You just do it," Mama said, and he still had no name. He had nothing but secondhand clothes and the quilt, but it was a start, I figured. We laid him in one of the drawers in the oak dresser, and he smelled better than any potpourri ever could.

"No mother ever feels prepared," Mama said, smoothing back my hair. "But when God gives you a job, he gives you the tools, as well."

"Oh, Mama, I need so many tools."

She laughed. "Listen to me. You can do all things through Christ who gives you strength. Not through you—through him—and this is something you repeat over and over, when your baby won't stop crying, when you're so tired you're about to fall over, when you look at him and don't feel the love you think you're supposed to feel. You can do all things, through Christ, who gives you love, who gives you patience, who gives you rest."

I cried when she went home. I cried and then made myself a cup of tea in Mrs. Bailey's kitchen and kept listening for my new son to wake, afraid to leave him even for a minute, and I wondered if I'd ever have time to myself again. And he still had no name, and I had no energy to do anything but sleep after sipping my tea. He woke only once, and as I fed him a bottle filled with cow's milk, his hands orchestrating the air and his eyes scoping mine, I felt something stir inside, a similar stirring to the one I'd felt in church when I heard Oliver sing. Even after the bottle was emptied we continued to stare at each other, as though witnessing something holy.

I moved home one week later because I needed Mama more than ever before. In my mind, I wasn't a mother. She was. And I needed her to teach me. And Mrs. Bailey was sad, but she gave me a basketful of muffins and I gave her the month's rent anyway, because she'd been so good to me and I didn't want to leave her high and dry.

Not three days later, a hand-carved crib appeared on my parents' doorstep, with a note attached to one of the maplewood rungs: "I thought you could find a use for this," in Oliver's cursive. I didn't hesitate to haul it into my room and fill it with soft sweaters and cover it with a cotton sheet.

I named my baby Shane. Hebrew, meaning God is gracious. And I wasn't sure how he was gracious except for the curl of a finger around mine, except for the milk burps and the quiet cooing and the wrinkling of his forehead and the trembling of his lip. Except for the way my heart hurt when he hiccupped, and the way I couldn't stop kissing his soft cheeks, I never knew I could love like this.

I still rose once or twice a night to feed Shane a bottle, and those times were tiring but sacred in a moonlit, silent sort of way, broken by the quiet slurping of nourishment and then the huddled motion of burping and sighing and falling back to sleep and sometimes I let him sleep with me in bed, but most of the time, he slept in Oliver's crib. It was a rocking crib, and I sang so many songs those first few months, for the way Shane's green eyes followed my face as though reading the love written there, and sometimes I felt so guilty I wept violently. For the love Nancy should have shared with her son. For a life I hadn't known I wanted. For the exhaustion of it all.

I still worked as a midwife, and Mama watched Shane while I did, because it was nice to have something else to do, and there was a baby boom, and I still shared the quilt. But as the weeks went on, I found it harder to be away from Shane. And the quilt was now his. He slept with it every night and lay on it during the day in a patch of sunlight on the floor of the living room, and Mama fussed over him and washed and folded his tiny clothes and knit him toques and sweaters while Daddy read Scripture to him.

Funny how a baby will make a family out of you. One day near Christmas, when Shane was just over one month old and we were all gathered in the kitchen having supper, someone knocked at the door. I went to answer it with Shane in my arms, and there he stood, looking shy beneath his blond hair and holding a bag.

"Hi, Clara," Oliver said, and then Shane gurgled and I laughed awkwardly.

"Hello," I said. "Would you like to come in?"

I had forgotten how tall he was. It had been weeks since I'd seen him at church.

"I'm afraid I can't," he said. "I just came by to say good-bye and to give you some . . . well, some wooden knickknacks I made for Shane."

He held out the burlap bag to me. "What do you mean, good-bye?" I asked.

I handed Shane over to him and took the bag where I found wooden rattles and a train set and a wooden cup, ball, and dog.

"I've found work in Pennsylvania doing carpentry," he said, and Shane was enamored by Oliver's nose. "I'm leaving first of January."

I felt my heart plunge even as I tried to sound casual. "Really? Oh . . . Please, come in for a minute. Mama's made the finest roast."

Oliver looked at Shane. "What do you think, buddy? Just for a minute, maybe?"

He followed me in and down the hall to the kitchen crowded with table and chairs and biscuits and gravy and roast, and Daddy stood and gave Oliver a hug and Mama found him a chair right next to me. And the whole time he sat, our elbows kept bumping for the closeness of it all. And I can't say I wasn't pleased.

He smelled like cedar, and his nails were clean and his palms, calloused, and he bounced Shane on his knee while he ate because Shane would go to no one else.

And even while Daddy congratulated Oliver on the new job, I knew Mama was watching me. It was as though she was making tea and staring out the window. My face was her sky, and I wondered what she saw in it.

And I suddenly wondered if he loved me anymore, and why I cared, and I wanted desperately to run up to my room.

When the coffee cups were drained, Oliver pushed back his chair and I swallowed, knowing this was it. Shane bawled shamelessly when I took him, and I wanted to say, "I know how you feel."

And then Oliver was at the door hugging Mama and telling her what a wonderful meal and shaking Daddy's hand. Then he turned to me and said, "Clara," and I nodded. My heart stuck in my throat.

"Thank you for the toys, Oliver," I said, shaking his hand.

"You're welcome."

Then he was walking out the door when, "I love you."

There was an awkward pause. Mama mumbled something about the dishes and Daddy said he'd help her.

They left us alone, and Oliver was looking at me. "What did you say?" his voice a whisper.

My face was hot. "I love you," I said again, Shane squirming in my arms.

He stepped toward me, and the door swung shut. "Really?" he said.

"Mmm." I couldn't believe this was happening and he was so close now, I could have buried my face in his plaid shirt. I didn't dare look up for what I might see. Why had I said anything? What was I thinking?

Then he was taking my chin and I couldn't help but look up and he was kissing me. I swear Shane laughed out loud in my arms.

16

The wedding was something to sing over, one week after Christmas, like a beautiful piece of art, and we married in Daddy's church. A simple affair, Mama stitching me an ivory dress with long flowing sleeves, and I carried red roses. The long kind with thorns because part of me wanted to know if this was all real.

I walked down the aisle on Daddy's arm, and he wore a new suit for the occasion and couldn't stop smiling. Mama was teary at the front in a stunning black-and-white dress with a lace collar and a wide hat. She'd always wanted one of those fancy hats "like Ava Gardner," she said, and she finally had one, her only daughter getting married at last, and Shane in a white gown in her arms, asleep.

And even as I walked down the aisle and the townsfolk smiled and nodded because who can resist a good love story, even as I looked up front and saw Oliver standing there in brown tweed with a bow tie and his hair slicked down and his hands in front of him, even as the piano played "The Wedding March," I could see the pieces of the quilt forming: the patches of my life, all there, and God sewing them together with tender threads. A child who needed a mother, a woman who needed love, and a man with a heart and a home.

After Daddy had read 1 Corinthians 13 and we'd sung some more hymns and signed the registry, we kissed. Then it was laughter and rose petals and me carrying Shane down the aisle and outside, the weather anointing us with white confetti snow.

I had learned, just weeks earlier, that Oliver had no family. His father had been drafted to World War I and had died in combat. Oliver had been his father's only child and had watched his mother die of the influenza when he was eleven. They had lived in the projects in Atlanta, Georgia, and after his mother passed away, his grandmother had taken him in and raised him to the best of her ability. But she was always forgetting things, and it got worse as the years went on until she was forgetting where she lived and Oliver was taking care of her, earning money with a paper route and then working in a factory at nights and doing school during the day until one day when he was gone, she forgot to shut the oven off. And the one-bedroom bungalow they lived in burned down, with her inside it. That's when Oliver enlisted. He was seventeen. He spent six years at war, became a decorated soldier, and came back with a limp. He moved to Smithers because it was small and he could start over. He could live off his army pension and begin a new life, and he rarely spoke of his family.

Our wedding had no reception, no gifts, no honeymoon, because we had to pack and move to Pennsylvania in just a few days, and all we wanted, following the ceremony, was to be together, alone. In Oliver's stone house.

Mama had packed us a picnic basket full of roast chicken, cornbread, and potato salad because, "The last thing you need on your wedding night is to have to make supper," and Mrs. Bailey had baked us brownies.

With Shane at Mama's house for the night, we spread a tablecloth on the carpet in the living room and sat beside each other awkwardly, still in our wedding clothes, and we opened up the basket, the fire making all sorts of sparks and the wind blowing winter against the windows.

And I wasn't hungry for food, but we ate anyway, and then we held hands up the stairs to the bedroom. I'd never been in Oliver's room before, and the bedframe was hand-carved, with flowers and hearts crawling up the top toward the center.

A large window overlooked the garden, just a bare patch of snow with stalks of hollyhocks dried out and waving. I stood by the window and held onto the curtain. Then I felt his arms around me and you probably don't need to hear this, Noah, except to say, we loved each other that night. And it's not how the movies say it is, but it's beautiful just like any relationship is: in its own messy kind of way, the kind that needs the protective circle of a wedding ring. There's pain in losing yourself this way, but there's love in the gaining.

And he held me for a long time afterward.

We began to pack.

And I cried, a lot, over those cardboard boxes, not ready to go to Bethlehem, Pennsylvania, with a man and a baby.

But Mama and Daddy reminded me it was only a state away, a four-hour drive, and they would be there once we got settled, they said. Daddy wiped his eyes with a blue checkered hankie and ever since Shane's birth, Daddy had needed a handkerchief. As though he'd sprung a leak.

And we stacked boxes like bricks in the back of Oliver's truck, and I drove my twenty-five-dollar car, Shane in blankets on the backseat. Like mad men, we drove, because if we looked back we feared we'd turn to salt.

As we drove, Daddy's voice ran through my head, through the car windows, through the flash of fields and signs and highway outside my window, the passage about charity. The one saying, *Charity suffereth long, and is kind; charity envieth not; charity vaunteth not itself, is not puffed up, Doth not behave itself unseemly, seeketh not her own, is not easily provoked, thinketh no evil.*

I'd been seeking myself for so long I didn't know where to look anymore.

So I looked instead at the back of Oliver's head in the truck, and his broad shoulders, and I followed him in my car and began to see a man I could trust. And maybe I wouldn't have to go through the pain of losing him.

Maybe somehow our love would outlast all of the others, or Jesus would come back before one of us died, or we would die together in each other's arms.

But for now, we lived, and I held onto the thought as tightly as I held onto the wheel.

Our new home was tall and stately with white siding and green shutters, just a walk away from the furniture store where Oliver would be working.

The town of Bethlehem was bustling. Women in hats everywhere, fancy hats, the kind Mama wore for my wedding, only they wore them every day, and they had dogs on leashes and sipped cocktails at cafés and sent their servant girls or nannies to the market for groceries.

I wasn't sure I didn't want to up and move back to Smithers, but I bit my tongue. Bought myself a hat. Made Oliver his favorite kind of sandwich every time he came home for lunch—tuna on rye—and asked him about his day and did the homemaker thing: folding towels, putting them away, washing diapers, putting them away, rearranging furniture and putting away clothes, and trying to make our empty house a home, with all of its space. But then one day I pricked my finger. Just a small prick on the edge of a safety pin, and it bled all over Shane's diaper.

And I sat on the couch we'd bought secondhand from Mr. Leung's down the street and held Shane and sobbed until I thought the house would fill from my tears.

And then I did something so familiar it made me feel much better. I made myself a cup of tea, and I thought of Mama and how she'd moved to Smithers not knowing anyone, just knowing her husband had a job there, and if Mama could do it, I could, too.

So I made a list of ways to get involved, hoping maybe I could make friends. Things like visit the local shops with Shane; visit the local churches, museums, and cafés. Read the newsletters and find a way to get invited to tea functions and socials. Make a pot of soup and take it down to the mission.

The list became long, and by the time it was done I had an ink stain on my finger, and Oliver was home, smelling of wood shavings and blowing kisses on Shane's belly.

"And how are you, Clara?" he said, stepping across the living room floor, with its hardwood and throw rugs, to where I sat at the dining room table. I showed him my list, and he nodded. "It looks good, honey. Which one do you think you'll start with?"

I rose. "The soup, I think. It's easiest. Shane and I will take it downtown in the car and hopefully a mission there can use it. I'll get supper—you rest," and so he sat down and played with Shane while I got roast beef on the table, while outside, street lamps played games with the shadows.

—∞∞—

I took soup down the next day to the Bethlehem Mission where veterans from the war found supper, shaky at the tables, and wobbled forks or spoons into mouths. I took it and served it, Shane the highlight of the night, gurgling and playing with silverware and making the saddest man smile.

I'd gone there looking for friends but ended up talking more to the vets than to any of the volunteers, Shane on my knee, long after the soup was gone. They told me stories about the war, and sometimes they became so agitated they had to leave and then come back and their eyes were very hollow. Like death had scooped out their joy.

We went back, week after week, with more pots of soup, and every time I went I forgot how lonely I was, for all of their emptiness.

But the other days of the week, I remembered.

I sat in our big new house and thought about Eva, about her yellow hair that looked like birds' wings when she ran, and how it had felt to laugh with someone. I thought about Miracle Martha and wondered how she was doing with her grandmother. I baked brownies and cookies and muffins, and I ate a lot of my baking. And soon my dresses felt snug, and I felt worse for it all.

"No wonder no one likes me," I said one day into an empty bowl, my stomach so very full.

And then the letter came.

July 24, 1951, it came.

A letter from Mattie, originally addressed to Clara Wilson at Smithers, Maryland, and Mama must have forwarded it on.

Shane was napping in his crib upstairs, and the afternoon was pooling light on the living room floor. I tucked an afghan around me and made a cup of tea. Then I sat on the couch with the afghan and contemplated not opening the letter, just keeping it, and feeling very loved, but reason overcame sentiment and I tore it open.

Dear Clara,

I hope this isn't too bold of me, but I've been thinking about you and wondering how you are. If you're not much of a letter-writer, please don't feel as though you need to respond. I just felt the need to write.

I should let you know I am no longer living in the house you visited me in. I moved because it was too hard. I needed a fresh start, and I am now living in a little apartment in downtown New Orleans and still working as a librarian. And I love it. I love the fresh scent of books. The way they make me feel safe. The way I can trust them to always be there, to hold me with their words. I know it sounds silly, but it's been the best way to heal. To be around stories, to remember in spite of losing Gareth, I'll always have his legacy.

So how are you? Are you making use of the quilt? I imagine you are married now, with kids. I do hope you'll consider writing, but please don't feel pressured to.

Sincerely,
Mattie.

I read it three times and drank my tea slowly and read it again. Marveling at how God had known, how he had sent me a friend through the post, and how a letter had been the very thing to introduce us in the first place.

And then I set down my teacup and pulled out some paper and a pen.

17

August 1953

Shane was two and a half and able to ride a tricycle, and it was all going too fast, this life.

The sun was making rainbows in the white linen curtains. I'd just given birth to Lula who lay wrapped in Mattie's quilt on the floor by the window while Shane was playing with her. Talking to her about the blueberries he'd just eaten, his mouth still purple.

We lived near a host of blueberry bushes, in the woods surrounding Bethlehem, and we drove to them almost every summer with buckets and picked them by the bushel and ate them by the handful and it had been three summers now. I was making pastry and my hands were covered in flour when the telephone rang.

The big black phone was by the refrigerator, and I picked it up and held it against my ear as I pressed into the pastry.

"Hello?"

"Hi, Clara? This is Mattie. How are you?"

I fairly dropped the phone. "Mattie?!"

It had been two years of writing and there was a stack of her letters in a box in my closet and she was my closest friend in spite of not really knowing her.

But we'd never talked on the phone.

"It's so good to hear from you," I said, with Shane tugging at the hem of my skirt saying he had to go to the toilet and Lula crying in the living room where she lay wrapped in the quilt.

"Did I catch you at a bad time?" said Mattie, and her voice was exactly the way I remembered it to be, the way her words were too: sweet, like molasses, and it reminded me it was almost lunchtime.

"I, well, I really want to talk to you," I said, "but the kids . . ."

"I get it, I do. I'll call back in a bit. Don't you worry."

So we said good-bye, and I found myself a bit frustrated with the children, because how many times did I get the chance to talk on the phone with a good friend?

But then I breathed deep and remembered them for the miracles they were. I kissed their chubby cheeks and gently hugged them each in turn and then took Shane to the toilet and set them all at the long wooden table—the one Oliver had made us last year—and fed them some homemade bread and molasses, Shane's favorite. I tucked Lula in the crook of my arm and sang to her "Mary Had a Little Lamb" and "It Is Well."

Still, she fussed, so I nursed her in the glow of the afternoon. She fell asleep at my chest, her long lashes against her cheek, and I still remember the serenity of that moment: sitting in that rocking chair by the window, Shane playing with cars on the hardwood floor, and the rustle of the wind through the aspen trees.

I didn't want anything to change. Even though Mattie was my only friend (I had acquaintances in Bethlehem, women who invited me to tea and to functions, but I hated getting dolled up, my hair in a twist and my face made up), in this moment, life was divine. God was so very present in these children, in the wind, even in the rocking of my chair, and I thought I could die happy.

And then the phone rang again, and I lay Lula down in her crib. It was Mattie.

We got to talking about the weather and her job and the children, and then she paused.

"Go ahead," I said. "Tell me why you called, Mattie."

She laughed, and I pictured her standing tall in her simple dress with her lovely face.

"You know me too well," she said. "You see, you wrote about the quilt a while ago. You told me how you'd used it when you were a midwife to wrap around all those precious babies. And how it had helped your mama. And I have this girlfriend, Gabriele, whose mother isn't doing too well. Gabriele's brother, Nicholas, died in the war, and her mother has never really recovered and the family's tried everything. I, well, I thought maybe you and I could go visit her at some point and bring the quilt and just listen to her story, you know? Ask her questions about her boy. Then maybe offer to stitch his name on the quilt, too? To remember him?"

Shane was getting tired; I could see him twirling, and then he fell down and whimpered. I picked him up and thought of this woman, how it would feel to lose a son. And then I couldn't think about it anymore because it was too hard.

"Yes," I said into the receiver.

"Yes?" she said.

"I think we should do it. I think we should help this woman."

Mattie laughed again, and it was glorious and loud, and then she cleared her throat and lowered her voice considerably. "Oh dear, I'm in the library, and I really should go. But I'll call you later and we'll talk more, okay? Thank you, Clara. It will be so good to see you again. And I know this will mean the world to Gabriele's mom."

After she hung up I just stood there, staring out the kitchen window, the receiver in my hand.

Then I picked up my tired son, his arms wrapped around my neck, and I climbed the stairs slowly with him, lay down in bed beside him. His slow breathing against my neck, and he smelled like soap and bread and earth.

I cried, lying there, thinking about how little we could offer this woman: just a quilt, with her son's name on it, and how unfair it all was, this loss of something, someone, so great.

But even as I thought this, I remembered how Shane's own mama gave her life away so he could have his, how this had given me a family. And how death sometimes gave birth to something sacred.

I crept down the stairs, avoiding the creaky board that always gave me away, and I scooped blueberries into pie crusts and sprinkled sugar and slid the pies into the oven.

Then I sat down with a cup of tea in the rocking chair, the wind still blowing and the curtains still rustling but everything seeming changed now.

And funny how just as you begin to settle, you're made aware of someone's needs. And you're kept always alive, serving each other.

—◦◦◦—

I wore my fancy hat, the black one with the wide brim, and I put on lipstick, and my children barely knew me. Oliver danced around me like a schoolboy, and I laughed when he kissed my neck and then sighed because I had to leave. Checking my watch for the umpteenth time and hugging Shane more, I wrapped Lula tight in the quilt and some blankets and Oliver grabbed my suitcase. He was going to drive me to the train station, where I would ride the rails to California. Mattie was paying my way. She would pick me up at the station, then we'd go visit Gabriele's mother and sleep over at an inn before returning home.

Shane wouldn't stop crying when I got out of the car, and Oliver held him and said, "Don't worry, Clara, he'll be fine, just go, have a good time," and I wept my way onto the train, wondering what I was doing.

It was a long ride, and Lula and I slept a lot. I hid in the bathroom, all tiny and squished, to nurse. And when I wasn't sleeping, I was praying for Gabriele's mother and for God to use this quilt.

And I cried and felt a bit frustrated by it all, at the way I had to leave my son to do this. And then we were there, pulling up to the station with Mattie's shining face outside the window, and my tears all but disappeared for the love I saw there.

She was a flurry of kisses and hugs and took my satchel and suitcase and gushed over Lula who was beautiful, even as a baby.

"How was the ride?" she said, leading me to her yellow Volkswagen Beetle. "We slept most of the way," I said, Lula fussing and me propping her up to see the sights as we drove.

"I thought I would take you to the inn to freshen up before we meet Mildred—Gabriele's mother. Does that sound all right?"

⸺⁂⸺

Two hours later we had freshened up and were driving again, so many cars and bikes and shops. Palm trees lining the highway and beyond it, the ocean, and teenagers playing the guitar on the beach and roller-skating down the sidewalk.

Nat King Cole on the radio and the air seemed to smell of salt and coconuts. I stuck my hand out the window and felt for a minute like a bird.

"Thank you," said Mattie, turning to me now. "For coming. I know this is a big trip for you. And I know it wasn't easy to leave Oliver and Shane . . . so, thank you."

I squeezed her hand. "For you, anything," I said.

⸺∞⸺

Mildred Silverstein was in bed when we arrived.

Her oldest daughter, Gabriele, answered the door. She lived down the street and spent most of her days here, she said, and her wide almond eyes were full. She couldn't stop thanking us. She was a small lady, almost disappearing inside of her black skirt and blouse, and the house was air-conditioned and silent.

So different from my noisy home with its fans and its windows wide open and Shane making car sounds and Lula crying.

She wasn't crying now, though. She was sucking on her fingers and staring at the brown-striped wallpaper, at the pink tasseled pillows in the living room, the couches covered in plastic.

We'd rested at the inn before coming, a quaint little place bursting with pink and purple blooms in the windows and smelling like strawberries. The sheets and toilet were clean, and that was what mattered, and the towels were soft. I'd given Lula a bath and made myself a cup of tea and wondered at how I was turning into my mother.

I'd spent some time massaging lotion into Lula's little body while her legs kicked the air, and then we'd napped a little, together, before Mattie had rapped softly at the door. And this was nice, I'd thought, being alone with my daughter, and I decided not to feel guilty anymore. It was good for us to spend time away. So I brushed my hair, pinched my cheeks, and walked to the car with the quilt in my satchel.

The wallpaper was old and curling at the edges as we walked the hall down to Mildred's room, Gabriele ahead of us, padding in moccasins. We got there and Gabriele went in first. Low mutterings, and then the door opened wide, and we stepped into a room full of glory.

Mildred was sitting up in a frilly white nightgown, and her hair was white, too. She looked like an angel with the sun pouring in through the window. The walls were yellow, there were daisies on her bedside table, and on her walls were pictures of her children. She had a thousand wrinkles in a small face, and she smiled so deeply when she saw Lula. "My, what a sweet child," she said in a singsong voice, and we drew close to this angel, to sit and chat a long while about Nicholas and his life and her life and her story.

I don't know if I've ever felt heaven more tangibly.

And where Gabriele saw a poor old woman losing her mind, I saw a doting mother celebrating her past. Delighting in bright colors and reading books and staring at photos of her children.

"He's not dead to me, you see," said Mildred. "He's right here," and she pointed to her heart, "and my husband is too, and I find I remember them better when I sit still."

When I showed Mildred the quilt, explained how Mattie had given it to me after Gareth died and how I'd used it to remember the lives of the children born after the war, I asked if I could honor Nicholas's life, too.

And she cried, pulling out an elegant ivory handkerchief and blowing her nose and then handing us each a daisy from her bedside table.

"You would do this?" she said, sniffing and glowing and Gabriele bringing in a tray of tea and cookies.

I pulled out my needle and thread then, and while Mattie and Mildred drank tea and talked more, and Gabriele held Lula, I stitched in the warmth of the window. And beneath Nicholas's name, I stitched, "celebrated."

Then I lay the quilt across Mildred's shoulders, and she laughed in a way that made me think she'd been holding it in for some time.

18

Mildred rose from bed and got dressed. It reminded me of the Bible story in which Jesus raises a woman from the dead and she turns around and waits on him.

And as we were sitting around Mildred's dining room table under a chandelier eating chicken and potatoes and drinking grape juice from wine glasses, Mildred, who'd put on pearls and a white cardigan over a rosebud dress, clapped her frail hands excitedly like birch leaves flapping in a breeze. Gabriele leaned forward, her eyes wide.

"Are you okay, Mama?"

"Oh, Gaby, I'm more than okay! I feel more alive than I have in a long time. When was the last time I made supper?"

Gabriele nodded. Pronged a potato. "I know, Mama. It's been, well, months at least."

Mattie and I looked at each other and smiled.

"I think you should talk to my friends," Mildred said then, and we both turned and stared at her.

"What do you mean?" I felt nervous and looked over at Lula, lying asleep in the living room wrapped up in the quilt. All I wanted was to go home and hug my family.

Mildred's pearls swung as she bobbed her head. "I have so many friends who've lost sons in the war and they know women, too, and how much room do you have on the quilt? Because we could fill it with names."

The quilt was suddenly so small compared to the need, and I wanted to curl up under it and hide.

But I smiled and nodded while Mildred chatted excitedly about the idea, and Mattie kept stealing glances at me.

After rhubarb crisp and nursing Lula and handing her to Mildred who took her to the backyard and sang to her in the dusk, Mattie and I went for a walk.

They lived close to a boardwalk that ran along the ocean, and we walked the beach, the tide rolling in.

We talked about Mildred and her pearls, and then Mattie stopped and turned to me. "Listen, Clara, we don't have to talk to anyone else. I just wanted to do Gaby a favor and visit her mother and help her know she wasn't alone. There will always be more people, there will always be so much need, and your family comes first."

I nodded. "I know." Swallowed. "I guess I need to talk to Oliver, you know? Part of me is just so tired, but I also don't want to say no, if this is what I'm meant to do. I mean, you gave me this quilt, and I want to honor Gareth with it."

We kept walking then, and Mattie's shoulders began to shake. We sat on the edge of the boardwalk then, and I put my arm around her, and in spite of her height, she seemed so small. And I prayed love would fill her, full.

"I just keep thinking it will get easier," she said, staring out at the water, at the seagulls dipping down and rising like washwomen, pinning up the waves. "I keep thinking maybe one day I'll find someone else, maybe have a family with him, but every time I meet someone or am introduced to someone I can only see Gareth. And I feel like I'm betraying him and . . . it's just so hard."

I kept my arm around her. Felt the weight of the war in her shoulders. My fingers clenching, for one man's hideous reign wrecking an entire generation of families.

"I think we should do this," I said then. "I'm not sure how, but over the next few years, we can visit families who've been hurt by the war and share Gareth's story with them and stitch their sons' or grandsons' names into the quilt. We'll fill every inch of space and remember them all."

The seagulls wove the sky and cried, their wings stretched out as they coasted the wind.

We visited with five of Mildred's friends during the week, five women whose sons had died in the war, and we told them of Gareth and "Amazing Grace" and stitched their sons' names. And many of them cried as though, for a moment, someone was holding their baby again and marveling at his beauty and saying, "You did a wonderful job, creating this life. Well done."

And when I finally arrived home one week after leaving, and Oliver was standing there on the train platform with Shane on his shoulders, I felt all of the love of God, saying, "Well done, my good and faithful servant," as I stepped off the train and fell into the arms of home.

19

Oliver was doing really well at his job, so well, in fact, that we were lacking nothing, and this, I felt, indicated a problem. Because we had no reason to need God anymore.

Life had fallen into a happy rhythm of babies and strollers and Oliver's roughened hands closing over mine at supper-time for grace. Shane was six now, in primary school, Lula was three, and Nellie had just been born.

We read stories at bedtime together, I helped Shane with his homework, and Oliver built us a chalkboard that I used to write the alphabet on.

The wind still blew through the aspens outside our window, and we had a lilac bush now and a flowering dogwood tree. I had been nominated head of the Women's Society in Bethlehem. Yet, some nights, in spite of everything, I cried into my pillow while Oliver snored beside me. For some reason, I missed Normandy and my knees in the dirt and the hum of airplanes overhead and the way life was very cherished there, kind of like chocolate, whereas now I always had a glass bowl full of them for guests.

It was an affluent time, and Bethlehem was booming. When Mama and Daddy came to visit, they made comments about our new love seat that had replaced our secondhand couch, about our rich mahogany furniture that Oliver had built. Mama rocked Nellie and looked out the window at our dogwood tree.

And I didn't know what to say or do. All I knew was I had no more time to serve at the soup kitchen for all of my committees.

They didn't visit us much, during this time, because they were moving from the diner—which had closed down for good—into a small two-bedroom apartment three blocks from the church. Daddy was still preaching and wearing the same wire-framed glasses, and Mama, her cardigans and slippers.

They'd raised me different, I knew, but I didn't know how to not spend money with it coming in the way it was, and with Oliver being so busy at work, all I had were my committees, my children, and our pink Cadillac. I had tried to buy Daddy and Mama a nice car, too, one of those fancy Chrysler convertibles to replace the broken-down Ford they'd bought used in the thirties, but they wanted nothing to do with our money or with nice things, they said. Daddy said nice things were from the devil, but I wasn't so sure.

We still went to church—a church like I'd been raised in—a tall, steepled affair with doctrine and hymns and an ancient congregation. And for three years now, Mattie and I had been meeting every few months to visit groups of elderly ladies across the United States and to hear their stories, stitching the names of lost loved ones into the fabric of the quilt.

Word had gotten out to the United States Veterans Association about it all—"Clara's Quilt" they were calling it, and Mattie didn't seem to mind—and they'd advertised about us, and women from all across the country were writing in and sharing their war stories and could we please come visit them?

We sorted through the letters and addresses and chose five every three months, who lived in the same area, to visit. And in spite of all my committees and the rich mahogany furniture, those were the only real times—besides caring for my children—when I felt worthwhile. When I knew God was smiling and my Mama, too, because this was holy work, this ministry, this quilt of love.

It was the smiles from women whose sons were killed in the front lines that saved me. It made Jesus very much alive and well and inside of me.

However, when I was at home late at night and Oliver was reading his newspaper by the fireplace and all I had was my knitting or my magazines, I often sobbed. Quietly, so no one would hear me, but one night Oliver did.

Nellie had just started to walk that day, and for some reason I couldn't let the baby in her go. I'd tried with everything in me to stall her from standing, and then from taking her first step, and what kind of mother does this?

Nevertheless, she was walking, and soon she'd walk right on out the door, right behind the others, leaving me all alone in this big white house with its hardwood floors and mahogany furniture. And I about broke down every time I thought of it, every time I saw her doing something new, when shouldn't I have been rejoicing?

One night Oliver heard me sobbing and put down his paper and stood up and walked over to the window where I sat in my chair. He put his hands on my shoulders and leaned forward, his hair against my head and said, "What's wrong, honey?"

I shook my head. I didn't want to tell him. He had enough on his mind with so much at work, and I was happy and didn't want him to think I wasn't. But here I was crying and so, "Nothing, sorry, I'm just tired, I think," I said. Then I rose and smoothed down my black-and-white-striped skirt and thought quietly about stepping off a bridge.

Then I realized I was in a very poor state indeed, and I put my head in my hands and said, "I think I need help."

We talked long into the night by the fire, Oliver's forehead wrinkled and him holding my hand and me confessing to it all: to not wanting to be on the committees and not wanting to live in this rich kind of way, but not knowing how else to do it. Wanting to be happy but terrified of being in a house by myself and trying to prevent Nellie maturing because of it.

"I didn't know," said Oliver, and I loved him so deeply in that moment for the mournful way in which he said it. I knew he was genuine. I knew it by the creases between his eyes, by the way he held my hand the whole time I talked, by the penitent way in which he sat.

"It's not your fault," I said. "You are doing so well at your work, and I'm so proud of you. I just want to be proud of me, too, and right now, I'm not."

"But I am," he said then, softly. "I'm so proud of the way you take care of our children. Of the way you make our home so warm and inviting, of the delicious suppers you prepare."

I leaned forward, imploring. "That's just the thing though, Oliver. I want more. I want to be more . . ."

"Than a mother? Than a wife?"

I could see I'd hurt him, but was it wrong to want to be significant as a woman, too, and not just in these other roles?

We stopped talking for a while, just watched the flames together, and then Shane called for some water. And when I came back, Oliver's head was in his hands.

I sat down, and he said, "I think I understand, and I'm sorry. I'm sorry for assuming you felt significant simply because you were serving my needs. Will you forgive me, Clara?"

Of course, I said, and forever, and always, and then we prayed together on the new brown shag carpet we'd put in the living room and we prayed God into the house, into our lives, into our hearts, into our children, whatever that might look like.

Later in bed we were both reading, and in the middle of a paragraph Oliver pulled his glasses off and looked at me. "You feel fulfilled helping women who've lost someone to war, correct?"

"Right," I said. "And the quilt is almost completely filled, and there are so many women who need help. Why?"

He paused. "Well, God has blessed us with this money, and I just wonder if maybe we can put it to better use. Maybe we can use it somehow to help those women, or people who were affected by the war, or something."

I nodded. "Yes. Money isn't the problem. It's how we're using it, and right now I feel it's all being spent in an empty kind of way. Maybe we could create some sort of scholarship or foundation or something. . . . And it wouldn't just have to be families of soldiers. It could be Jewish relatives who have been affected."

Oliver laughed quietly. "I'm not bringing in *that* much money—but yes, it's the right kind of idea. There are so many ways to help people. Let's pray and sleep on it and see what comes to mind."

So we did, and it was one of the fullest, deepest sleeps I could remember having in weeks, and I woke up smiling.

20

2000

Clara pulled her sweater close. Her bones ached from the length of the ride; it was their third day driving, and they were passing through Tuscaloosa, Alabama. They were just over four hours away from New Orleans, Oliver said, his voice sounding fainter than usual, and he wanted to keep going if everyone was okay because they were so close. Shane called the others on his cell while Clara huddled in her cardigan.

She felt she would scream if she didn't get a break soon. They'd stopped for a mid-morning snack in Birmingham, just one hour back, eating crackers and cheese and the kids running and yelling and the sun splintering through the trees; but all too soon they were piling back into their cars, and she was just plain tired of driving. No one else was complaining, though, and Mozart was on the stereo and the sun was shining, and she had nothing to whine about, she told herself.

"So, this foundation, or scholarship idea . . . what became of it?" Noah said. He and Shane had switched seats again, Noah beside her now. She was honored by the way they'd been all ears this whole trip, leaning in to hear her story and not interrupting once, not since breakfast in Chattanooga, Tennessee.

"Well, it seemed ridiculous at first . . ." she began, when . . .

"Dad, are you okay?"

Shane's profile was pale as he was staring at Oliver, and Clara suddenly noticed her normally attentive husband huddled over the wheel, and the car, crawling.

"I can't see . . ." was all he could say, and horns were blaring behind their van and Clara's knuckles turning white as she gripped the door handle.

"Pull over, honey, can you do that?" she said, unbuckling her seatbelt and putting a hand on Oliver's shoulder.

He slowly turned the wheel and parked on the side of the road with the hazards flashing, and soon the family lined up in vehicles behind them.

Oliver remained stooped while the rest of the family crowded with questions and worried glances. Clara was beside Oliver, now, his face toward hers. He was normally brave, but this time, his pupils were like saucers.

"Call 911," she said, standing and directing the statement to no one; there was a flash of silver as cell phones were pulled.

Shane and Noah pulled Oliver from the van, and he curled up on Clara's lap and she stroked his gray hair. Everyone else sat down beside them on the side of the road, a silent string of DNA. Praying.

Soon the ambulance arrived, and Clara and Oliver rode in the back while the rest of the family followed behind. Oliver was moaning, and Clara was stroking his hand like she would a child. Singing, "Jesus, Tender Shepherd Hear Me" and begging Jesus to walk them through the valley.

———

They waited by the vending machine in the DCH Regional Medical Center in Tuscaloosa; the machine hummed, and

Clara found it irritating. She began to pace, and Lula and Nellie tried to comfort her in turn, but she would have none of it. No, she needed to walk and there was no comforting her, thank you, just pray, please. And so they all were bending heads, the little ones, too, when the doctor emerged in his lab coat and thick glasses.

"I'm wondering whom I should speak to regarding Oliver Flanagan?" he said. Clara stepped forward, and he looked at her.

"His wife, I'm presuming?" and she nodded.

"I'm very sorry, but your husband has suffered a mild stroke. It would be advisable for him to remain in here for a few nights before returning home."

Clara nodded again. It was all she could do at this point. "Will he be all right?"

"I believe he will be fine, but it's essential he get some rest. He'll be in room 307, but please don't visit all at once. Stress of any form can trigger a subsequent stroke."

The doctor looked down at his clipboard. "I'm sorry, but I must see to another patient. Please don't hesitate to contact any of the nursing staff should you have any questions."

Clara stood still while he turned and left, and the only word running through her brain was *stroke. Stroke. Stroke.*

Lula was standing beside her now and helping her to her seat, and Marie—Shane's middle girl, who was named after Clara's mother—sat on her lap and leaned against her chest. Clara found the words to repeat what the doctor had said, and then Shane went and talked to the nurses at the front desk for a minute while Nellie and Lula held Clara's hands. Shane returned, suggesting the others go and book a few rooms at the inn down the road and he and Clara would join them as soon as they could.

"I'm not leaving Oliver," Clara said then, and Shane said, "I know, Mom," even as the others kissed her, said they'd see her later.

She leaned heavily on Shane as they walked to Oliver's room and he didn't complain; he was such a good boy. Always had been, so kind and caring, and putting others first. He held the door open for her and it said 307. Oliver's room.

But there must have been a mistake. They'd switched Oliver with someone else, with someone much older, more haggard, with tubes hanging out of him. Then the man opened his eyes, and she saw Oliver, somehow stuck in this old man's body, and she couldn't get to him fast enough and she wanted to pull him out of there, out of his body, to save him.

But the nurses, the tubes wouldn't let her, and they were asking her to sit, please. But she couldn't because Oliver needed her, and they said no, they needed to take his blood pressure, and then Shane was leading her to a chair and she sat down like a wooden doll and stared at the wall. Wondering how she'd gotten there. Her, the founder of a nonprofit organization, unable to care for her own husband.

And across the room she saw him. He was looking at her, and then he smiled. His same, shy smile. All the way from over there.

She sat beside him all night long while he dozed in and out, with nurses coming and going, monitoring his pulse and checking his IV, and she wanted to tell them, *He isn't normally like this. My husband. He's strong. You should have seen him when I married him, he could swing an ax like nobody's business,* but they barely saw her there, in the corner, in her cardigan, and so she shrunk inside the knitted threads and crossed her ankles.

She shouldn't have let him drive. "I shouldn't have let him drive," she told Shane when he came the next morning smelling of coffee and carrying a paper bag full of muffins. She couldn't eat, she told him, but he gave her a blueberry one, anyway.

"It wasn't your fault," Shane said, as the muffin crumbled in her hand and she let it fall to the floor and he bent to scrape it up and sat down with a sigh. And she felt sorry for him. For causing him such stress, but she wore wrinkled clothes and felt very wrinkled inside, too, and "Mattie!" Oh dear, Mattie would be waiting, and them, not there.

Shane put a hand on hers. "Don't worry, Mom, I called her. You know Mattie, she was ready to come down here and save us all, but I told her just to sit tight because Dad is going to be better in no time, and then we'll be on the road."

Clara could have cried for the kindness in his eyes, and she patted his arm and coughed a little. "Thank you, son." And she wondered if they'd get to the museum in time to meet with the curator; they had a deadline to meet, and she wished with everything in her she hadn't crumbled the muffin.

Oliver was stirring now, on the bed, and she was beside him, singing to him, and he opened his eyes and smiled at her. "My angel," he said. "Do you know, I loved you since the first day I saw you?"

Clara swallowed. "You mean that day in church?"

Oliver shook his head slowly. "No, even before then, I saw you walking one day, toward the diner, and you walked with such a sense of purpose. Your red hair flashing in the sun. I fell hard for you."

Clara laughed, but she cried, too, inside, and said, "You were so quiet. I had no idea."

He nodded. "You had no idea how special you were. But I knew."

Then his head fell back against the pillow, and he sighed in a way that frightened Clara, and she begged him to stay alive.

"Don't worry, Clara-girl," he said, closing his eyes. "I'm not going anywhere without you."

The following night, Noah sat with Clara at Oliver's bedside.

She had dozed all day and was awake even as the moon rose. It poured light into the room and spilled across Noah's sneakers, and she wondered again why her grandson cared about a little old woman like her.

But he tucked a blanket around her shaking bones and slid his chair close to hers. For a while, they played Uno, and then, as Oliver's snores filled the room, he said, "So, Grandma, I'd really like to know the rest of your story. But if you're too tired, it's okay."

She had been staring at the floor, wishing she had something to knit or a crossword to do, when Noah said this, and she straightened her shoulders. "Yes, there's no time like the present," she said. "Where was I?"

"You were talking about starting a foundation or something . . ."

She smiled, nodded. Tucked the blanket closer. "Ah, yes, Forever Family—the organization we started. Well, I'll tell you Noah, I had no idea what I was getting into. But the Lord knew. He always does."

21

Spring 1956

It was that same spring, 1956, after I'd spoken to Oliver about wanting to do something selfless.

I spent days mulling and praying about how to use our money. *Maybe we could downsize,* I thought, *and live more simply and give more away,* and it was all so radical and invigorating I felt like singing.

So I did, I sang while I clothed the children and washed their hair. I sang while I made tea and bought the groceries. And I'd never felt more alive in that big white house in Bethlehem.

Impulsively, I quit being on committees and stopped going to tea socials, and I wore my hair down, red and wild. I threw away my lipstick and stopped saying things I didn't mean, just to get invited somewhere. Because I had a purpose other than being liked. I wasn't sure what it was yet, but I would know soon. I could feel it.

Then one day Mama was visiting me, Daddy gone to a church conference, and we decided to give some stuff to the mission. We went through the kids' closets and found pants and shirts and toys they didn't need anymore, and then Mama said it. She said, "Wouldn't it be neat to keep little snippets of things that belonged to a child, to preserve them somehow? Like a photo album of sorts?"

And I stopped, my arms overflowing with cloth and colors, and I said, "That's it!"

Shane turned from where he was playing with Legos. Lula hugged the doll in her arms, and Nellie clapped her hands.

"What's it?" said Mama.

"That's what we can do. We can get families to send in special memorabilia that belonged to the deceased, like a piece of cloth from a favorite pair of pants or patches from an old baby blanket or letters or poems or anything significant that reminds them of their loved one. And then a group of us volunteers can stitch those pieces into quilts and mail the quilts back to them."

I laughed outright with the possibility of this beautiful dream, and Mama was all smiles.

"It's perfect," she said in her quiet, reasonable way. "Just perfect."

At night, over supper, over ham and beans and potatoes, I told Oliver, and his eyes shone a little as he sliced his meat.

"I love it, Clara," he said. And then he paused. "But—and I'm not trying to be critical—I'm just wondering about logistics. Like where will you find the ladies to help you? And how much money will it take to purchase the fabric for the quilts? And will this be an official nonprofit organization or just a small volunteer movement?"

I dug into the potatoes. Lula was fussing and Nellie, too, and a bit of the light went out of the room, but then I looked across the table at Mama. And she just nodded once at me, a slow, firm nod, telling me everything would be all right.

"God will provide the answers," I said slowly, and as I said it, I believed it. The way you believe in a rainbow or a hug or the birth of a child. All of which follow hardship.

Oliver took my hand. "I'm sorry, I didn't mean to bombard you. And yes, I believe he will. I'm so proud of you, honey."

I could breathe again, and the children quieted, even as light returned.

—ⴲ—

Mattie came to our house for Thanksgiving, and while the world seemed to fall apart in colorful piles outside our windows, we slowly put it back together, from our chairs by the fireplace.

We talked and prayed, and Oliver and I, and Mattie, decided we would not sell the house. "Sometimes it's good to downsize, but it's also good to see what you've been given as just that: a gift," said Mattie.

I looked at the white linen curtains dancing in the breeze, and they suddenly seemed like angels, guarding our windows, and then I saw it: the tables and chairs and the women lining them and the fabric strewn across them and the blue and yellow baby quilt hanging on the wall, like a guardian, and the air electric with needles and thread and patterns and my own children watching, and it was all happening in our home. Like pieces of a promise, everything was taking shape: the money, the house, and Mattie, who knew how to quilt.

"Now all we need is to find some ladies to help us," said Mattie on the final day. She was dressed in her ivory felt jacket, her suitcase in hand and Oliver driving her to the station. It was Monday, and she was back to work the next day, and I wanted to keep her here, somehow.

"Yes . . ." I had three kids pulling at my skirt and suddenly felt very tired. "Where will they come from?"

Mattie knew me enough to say, "God will provide."

Oliver carried her suitcase to the car, and the children and I waved for a long time at the window, waved until all we could see were our hands, and then we just sat and held one another, all kind of piled on top of one another, the way you do when you miss someone.

And suddenly I remembered I was the mother and could make them feel better, and so I did. We made plaster hands, mixing up flour and water and cups of salt, and then we pressed our hands into it, laughing as Nellie ate some and Lula got it in her eyebrows, and we placed the prints on the windowsill to dry.

Then I pulled frozen strawberries from the freezer and heated them on the stove, and we ate them with sugar. And Shane asked where the sugar went because he couldn't see it, and he wanted more, please, but I explained to him it was still there. It had just dissolved.

"What's dee-solved?" he said.

I thought for a minute. "You know how we know God is real, but we can't see him?"

"Like how we pray to him, and he helps us, but I can't hug him goodnight?"

"Yes, exactly. Well, I guess God is kind of like sugar. He dissolves inside our hearts. So he's there, and he's making us sweeter, so to speak, but he isn't visible."

There was quiet as they ate, and I thought about the love of Oliver and these children and the friendship of Mattie and the dream of the women at the tables, and I thought, in fact, God *is* so very visible. We just have to have eyes to see him.

Not two weeks later, Mattie mailed a letter to the United States Veterans Association explaining our dream to start a quilting bee for the families of deceased soldiers, and one week after that (seven days before Christmas) the news was in magazines and papers across the country—*The New Yorker*, the *Chicago Tribune*, the *Washington Post*—and we had reporters traipsing up to Bethlehem with snow on their boots to visit the house that would become home to Forever Family, which was the name Mattie and I had chosen.

It was a Christmas miracle, I told Oliver after the reporters had gone and the kids were in bed, and he laughed and held me, and outside the kitchen window we could see the glow of the Nativity at the town square.

We drove to Maryland December 23 to get away from it all, to have a quiet Christmas with Mama and Daddy, and to feel the closeness of Jesus as we unwrapped presents. Oliver had carved me a wooden sign that said Forever Family, and I gave him new reading glasses; the children each received one toy. And we sang carols late into the night and then attended church the next morning, Christmas morning, to hear Daddy give the Gospel story. The one story I never tired of. The story of a baby who died for the world.

And I thought about God's loss. I thought about it, sitting there in the pew beside Oliver and Shane and Lula and Nellie and Mama, how he could have thought of another way to save the world but chose to give up something so dear as his only son.

I thought about how I'd nearly refused to accept the gift of family for the fear of losing them. How we are all God-in-flesh, born to die to ourselves, so others might be saved.

"Make me willing to lose," I said in a hushed prayer while standing to sing "O Come, All Ye Faithful."

Yet those days it seemed all about gaining, us arriving home later in the week and unable to open the front door for the canvas bags full of mail sitting in front of it. Letters, from mothers and fathers and wives and sisters and brothers and uncles and aunts across the country, telling us of their loved ones lost to war or lost to an injury or sickness acquired at war or lost mentally or spiritually, and everyone was represented: Jewish, American, French, and English. Mattie flew in, this time, from New Orleans to help me sort through the mail during her Christmas break.

The mail was in response to the articles in the journals, and they didn't stop. And Mattie and I, we just read and read, fed the children and read, and prayed and read.

"How do we choose?" I said. "How do we know which ones to make quilts for?"

Mattie paused. Lula was sitting in her lap and reached out a hand to cup Mattie's calm face. "We pray some more. And then we select a number—we decide how many quilts we can afford to make over the next year. And then we decide which families seem to be hurting the most, and we start with them."

So we did. We prayed, and then we chose.

It was hard, but we kept the other letters, should time and money and resources arise, even as more bags of correspondence arrived, and they wouldn't stop. We put out notices around town for ladies with quilting experience, ladies who wanted to donate their time to this cause; and we asked them to meet at my house on January 23 if they were interested. And on that day the living room was full. Women of all ages came, some with bent backs, others with tall thin necks, some with shy eyes, and others with loud laughs. We served scones and Earl Grey and talked; we decided to meet two days a week to make the quilts.

It was all coming together, these pieces, and I felt a surge of something big. Something so much bigger than all of us, giving birth in a small town called Bethlehem.

22

2000

Oliver stirred, and Clara stood over him, hand to his fore-head, and she thought maybe she should tell the nurses she was one, too—a certified nurse. It had been years since she'd practiced, but she still remembered how to soothe a fever and check for a pulse and monitor breathing, and Noah just sat back and she was glad. She could only take care of one person at a time these days, and she should have paid more atten-tion to Oliver. Should have seen the way he was wilting at the wheel, and why had she let him drive?

Yet, she knew it was his way of taking care of her, of them, because even though he had a prosthetic arm, he could still do that, he said, and she knew she needed to let him. He had practiced for thirty-five years, relearning the wheel, and he needed to feel useful. No one dared say anything about it. But now, she realized, she should have.

And all of a sudden a hand was on her arm, and she jumped a little. "It's okay, Noah, I'll be fine, thanks," she said without turning.

"Hi Clara," said a woman's voice, one she knew very well, and Clara found herself staring into the round, smiling face of Mattie.

"I came as soon as I heard," said Mattie, smelling of chamomile tea and pulling Clara close. She wore a crimson scarf around her neck, and her gray hair hung to her shoulders.

"You look so elegant," said Clara, glancing down at her rumpled shirt and skirt. Then she sighed and smiled. "And you didn't have to come! But I'm so glad you're here."

They stood, side by side, staring down at Oliver in the midnight hour, watching his chest rise and fall.

"How is he?" Mattie's voice was soft.

She had never remarried. She always said she was married to the library, with its books that didn't talk back to her, and she would laugh as she said this, but Clara wondered. And even now as she looked into her friend's gentle face she saw an ancient sorrow.

"He's not well," said Clara, tucking the sheets around Oliver's chin and wishing she could erase his worry lines. The way he looked, the color of ash. "The doctor says he's had a mild stroke and that he'll have to spend a few days here."

The door shut behind them, and Clara turned, realizing Noah had slipped into the hall leaving these old friends to talk.

"He let me in," said Mattie, following her gaze. "You were so preoccupied you didn't notice, but he sure cares about you. You can see it in his eyes."

Clara nodded, turning back toward Oliver. "He takes after his father. Such good hearts."

Mattie took off her scarf and laid it across one of the chairs in the room, then pulled up another chair, and they both sat at the side of the bed.

"How did you do it?" said Clara, turning to her friend. "How did you stay so strong after Gareth died?"

Mattie twisted the gold band on her finger. "Oh, Clara, you don't know the half of it. I have been so dishonest with you. For a while, I was so angry I couldn't see straight. I was so young. I actually quit the church because I couldn't believe in God anymore. I mean, I believe in him now, but for a while I felt so alone. Like God had gone and forsaken me—the one thing he'd promised to never, ever do. And all Gareth and I had ever done was give our lives for him. For this God we couldn't see, and this was how he repaid us? So quite frankly, I didn't see why I needed him."

A nurse came in, checked Oliver's vitals, then left again.

"Go on," said Clara gently. "I want to hear it all."

Mattie sighed. "I've never told anyone this. I've never confessed my doubt, not even to a priest although I'm not Catholic, but at one point I thought about going to mass just so I could light a candle for Gareth. It seemed so right, to be able to do one small thing for him. I even liked the idea of getting all my sins out into the open. But instead, I just asked for more hours at the library. Because all I was doing in my silly apartment was looking through old photos and letters from him and crying. I wasn't eating or sleeping, and I certainly wasn't praying. Then one day I fainted when I tried to stand, and when I came to, I realized I hadn't had anything to eat in four days and hadn't showered in over two weeks. It was time to do something. So I started going to church again.

"I was reading a lot of the stuff Gareth used to read, like *The Problem of Pain*, and trying to figure out how religion and suffering mixed," said Mattie. "I really missed church, you know, the singing and believing in something bigger than yourself, believing there is meaning in spite of it all. And even though

I was still angry, I was starting to realize war and suffering made God sad, too. And that helped."

Then Mattie coughed and smoothed her dress over her knees and took Clara's hand. "I have to ask you to forgive me," she said.

Clara tried not to look surprised. "For what?"

"Well, I was angry at you, too."

"You were?"

"Yes, I was hurt—and a bit jealous—because you got to be the last person to see Gareth. And, well . . . a little bit angry you couldn't save him. And I know it wasn't right of me," Mattie said hurriedly, gripping Clara's hand, "but it's just how I felt at the time, you know? I'm so sorry."

Clara was confused and tired. She withdrew her hand and busied herself with Oliver's blankets, but she felt too full of emotion. She had to swallow a few times before she said, "I'm sorry I couldn't save your husband. This is a lot to take right now, and I'd like to be alone with Oliver, if that's okay . . ."

The room was suddenly cold and quiet, and out of the corner of her eye Clara saw Mattie hang her head. "I'm sorry. You're right, I shouldn't have said anything. I'm so sorry, Clara," and the chair scraped. Footsteps and the door closing, and silence.

And for a few minutes Clara readjusted Oliver's blankets and then collapsed into her chair and wept. While Oliver breathed in and out and the IV made a sort of swishing sound.

No one was around when she emerged from the room, half an hour later. The hospital halls were like long white roads in an otherwise black night. A few patients wandered by, dazed, and then some nurses in their clean leather shoes, and the whole world seemed to be sleepwalking.

Clara cried some more in the elevator. She took it down to the front entrance of the hospital. The clock on the wall struck 1 a.m., right next to an oil painting of a man and his wife. *They must have founded this place*, she thought. They looked happy.

She needed to get away. She shuddered to think it, this wife needing to escape her husband and her family, but she craved space. Away from the smells of antiseptics, away from a husband who wouldn't wake up, away from the reminder of her conversation with Mattie, away from anyone who might ask questions.

She'd been half-expecting to see Mattie when she emerged from the room. Or Noah, even. But no one was there. And she wondered where Mattie had gone.

Why had she gone and been so rude to a friend who'd driven all this way? A friend who'd confessed her thoughts only to be shunned? And Clara stood gazing out into a night of city and sky and wondered if maybe she should go for a walk.

The streets were bright with street lamps, like miniature moons lighting her way, and she nodded at their friendly glow as she passed. She looked up and saw offices still lit and wondered who might be working at this hour and where their families were. Where was her family? In a hotel, waiting for her, and Oliver in a hospital bed with tubes, and she huddled against the cold of it all, against the way she'd hurt and was hurting. She wondered who she was to think she could withhold grace.

After all, she would have been angry, too, if the roles had been reversed.

Clara found a canal with wooden benches and sat staring at the water, at the moon doing tango with the waves. How uncertain, this life. And this is why she'd never wanted to get married in the first place—for the agony of finding that marriage huddled over a wheel, unable to move.

But she hadn't just gotten married. She'd gotten motherhood and grandmotherhood. She'd gotten children and grandchildren. She'd gotten wisdom and its sisters, fear and humility, and she'd gotten Forever Family, with its ladies stitching legacies across America.

And she'd gotten Oliver.

Her hands trembled, recalling the night he'd first held them. The night she'd said yes and he'd looked at her. "I will never leave you, till death do us part, Clara Anne," and she had believed him. And he hadn't.

But she had left him alone in a strange hospital, and how could she? When he needed her most? He could be waking up, even now, and she stood so quickly the blood rushed and she steadied herself on the bench, wobbled, then drew up to her full five-foot-two and began to retrace her steps.

Soon she didn't know where she was, with these tall houses and wide gardens and limousines and gates, and she was so tired. Perhaps she should stop and ask someone for directions, but who would be awake at this hour?

Eventually she decided to sit on the curb and rest a little, until her ankles stopped throbbing, and maybe she'd lay her head on the grass, too, and close her eyes, and only for a minute or two. Only until she could focus on where she was and gain her bearings and maybe she would just sleep a little.

Clara stared into the faces of her family. Lula was crying, and Shane and Noah were picking her up and carrying her somewhere, laying her down. The cushions felt so soft she wanted to say thank you, that she would be all right, and not to worry, but instead she drifted back to sleep.

Noah was missing.

Clara shook her head, and the picture came into focus. She was in Oliver's hospital room. They must have brought a cot in for her, and Oliver was sitting up, propped by pillows, and she must be dreaming, she thought. He was still pale, but he was awake, and looking at her. She tried to say something, but everyone was talking about Noah.

"What happened?" she said, squeaking, and they all turned.

Shane said, "After they brought you back last night, we all went off to bed. Then, this morning, we found a note from Noah, saying not to worry; he was going somewhere to do something important and he would contact us soon."

"But where? Where did my son go?" Beth was walking back and forth with Elise asleep in her arms. Shane tried to put his arms around her, but she pushed him away. "It's too much, Shane, just too much. Just get my son back. I'm going to the hotel. Come on Marie."

So they left, Marie crying and saying she wanted to stay with Daddy, and Shane begging Beth not to go. Clara sat up on the cot and took Oliver's good hand.

It wasn't as shaky as before. "I'm feeling stronger, now, Clara," he said. "I'm sorry for scaring you."

She nodded. Squeezed his fingers. "It's okay. I'm sorry for scaring you, too."

"Are you all right?" he said then. "I heard Mattie was here . . . where did she go? And why did you fall asleep on someone's lawn?"

She swallowed. "It was horrible, Oliver. I was horrible. She drove all this way and confessed something. She said she'd been angry, years ago, because I hadn't saved Gareth, and could I forgive her? And I asked her to leave."

Oliver didn't say anything.

"Now the curator won't get his quilt, because we were supposed to meet him today. And Mattie's not going to forgive me for not forgiving her, and Noah is missing, and it's all so awful, Oliver. I've messed everything up."

He held her then, the rain slapping against the window. And she thought this must be what God feels like. All safe and warm and dry. In the middle of a storm.

23

They huddled together in Oliver's hospital room, a web of women praying and men mulling while Shane kept trying Noah's cell. And eventually Beth returned with deli sandwiches and puffy eyes.

"He's never done this sort of thing before," she kept saying. "He's always been such a good boy," and Shane broke in with, "He's not necessarily being a bad boy right now, Beth. We just don't know what is going on."

Clara was twisting her hands together, wondering if she had caused this. Her, with her life story and her fight with Mattie and Noah's heart absorbing it all.

Oliver's face was blanching so they tucked him into bed and turned down the lights. "This place makes me feel sicker," he said. "All of these smells and these white walls—it's like a place someone goes to die, and I'm not ready to die."

The grandchildren were running up and down the halls and then into one another and blubbering and wailing and Clara decided to take them for ice cream. "I'll come with you," said Nellie.

"I can do it, you know," Clara said, pulling on her cardigan and stepping into her loafers. "I know I got lost last night, but the ice cream shop is right around the corner."

"I could use some fresh air, though. Is that okay?"

Clara nodded and suddenly felt tired, leaning on Nellie's arm as they followed an excited clan of children to the shop, and the breeze lifted their hair and the edges of their spirits.

"Sometimes all it takes is something to look forward to," said Nellie, the kids dancing around them and singing, "Ice cream, ice cream, let's get some ice cream!"

"You mean, hope?" said Clara, looking at her daughter, at the way her face looked like Oliver's, at the gentle line of her jaw and the long curve of her nose.

Nellie nodded. "Hope. Yes. Noah's letter was a glimmer of hope. It tells us he's got a purpose right now. And that changes everything."

The bell on the red-roofed ice cream shop clanged, and there was a jostle of arms as the children stood on tiptoes and peered in at the buckets. A gentleman with a white apron and a moustache smiled at them from the counter and waved his ice cream scoop.

Clara thought about this, about hope, even as they chose their flavors and their cones and filed out of the shop and then back in, when Elise's ice cream fell and her face, too. "One more, please," they said, and the man with the moustache looked tenderly at Elise who was crying and gave her an extra scoop and for free, too.

"And that was hope," said Nellie as they left the shop again. "The free scoop of ice cream, the gesture behind it, and it's everywhere. The chance to do life over, to try again."

Clara thought about this. About the way she had short-changed Mattie. About how she had refused to give her a second chance, because forgiveness is hope wrapped in humility.

The thing about forgiveness is, you have to accept it before you can give it, and she wasn't sure she had ever stopped blaming herself for those soldiers' deaths. The ones on her watch. And the babies, too, the ones who didn't make it, and even Shane's mother. Despite the gift Shane was, Clara was always holding him tighter for the way she felt she'd robbed him, and his mother, by not being able to save her.

They walked down the street toward an elementary school and a park, and Nellie and Clara sat on the bench while the kids sat on their laps and licked their cones. Then it was pushing them on the swings and catching them on the slides.

At one point, Elise flew down a red plastic tube and into Clara's arms and wrapped her arms around her neck, and smelled of bubble gum; and Clara felt the earth let out a long, quiet breath. Like everything had turned over and started fresh.

"Can we stop at the van for a second?" Clara asked Nellie as they walked back to the hospital, the children sticky and giggling.

"Yes, Mama, of course. Kids, come this way. Grandma needs to get something."

They arrived at the Caravan, and Clara opened the back and rooted around, beneath the umbrella and rain jackets and puzzles. Then she put a hand to her mouth.

"It's gone," she said. "The quilt is gone!"

They heard from Noah that night around a table at Samson's Pizza Shop, a quaint restaurant downtown with brick walls and wood-fired pizza ovens and lanterns hanging over the tables. The kids were stringing cheese and slurping soda while Shane was on the cell with his son.

"He's in New Orleans," said Shane, afterward, wiping at his mouth with his napkin. Standing up, he wrapped the leftover pizza while the kids protested. "He caught the train to the National World War II Museum because he knew you wouldn't be able to meet the curator in time."

"He took the quilt, then," said Clara, more to her napkin than anything.

Beth was already gathering up the children and praising God and clucking her tongue, and the others were rising and stuffing in final bites.

Shane nodded. "The curator has it. It's been accepted as an artifact."

Clara laughed. "That boy. Lord knows I needed him to do this, to get it there in time, to get all this straightened out."

Oliver smiled at her. He'd been released that afternoon with a prescription and a stern warning not to overdo it. Oliver had laughed at the time, but he wobbled now as he rose. "The Lord always knows, Clara dear. Shall we?"

And he held out his hand but ended up leaning on Clara as she guided him to the van.

24

They drove over four hours to Louisiana, Oliver beside Clara in the back, Shane in the driver's seat, Lula beside him, eating pumpkin seeds. A man named Bon Jovi on the radio was "Living on a Prayer," and *Isn't this all we're ever doing?* Clara thought. *Living on a prayer? The dream of something better, the hope of Someone divine hearing us?*

After a while, Oliver fell asleep, and Clara stroked his fake hand, the rough contours and grooves, and it all felt so real, his prosthetic.

"You were just a little thing, still," Clara said, touching Lula's shoulder, who turned down the music, "maybe seven years old. You had started school."

"Is this when Dad cut off his hand?" Lula said, turning to look at her mother.

"He had been using one of the new blades, one of the fast ones, and someone had been calling his name in the shop or something and he'd looked up, and the saw just kept on going. All that blood. And me, a nurse, but I nearly fainted when they called me to the shop and the ambulance there, and I saw the pool where his hand lay and him, where he lay, unconscious, and I knew right then life would never be the same."

Lula turned the stereo off completely and said, "Tell me more, Mom."

Clara smiled.

"Well, as soon as I told Mattie, she came. She had been planning on coming anyway, she said, for her quarterly checkup on Forever Family. They still met in our house and shipped the quilts from the local post office and the women, coming two days a week. And then when Mattie decided to stay and help for six months, your father recovering on the couch, we decided we might need to relocate the nonprofit. What with Shane being nine years old, and Oliver being home all of the time, and Mattie living with us.

"None of you kids ever complained, but we needed some sort of family space. To remember who we were. You know, you can spill all messy and real across the pages for a while, but you forget what you want your lives to read like, and that is when you need to gather the words close, again. The people, the heart of the story, close. You take care of the people who make it all worth reading: your family. You two, and your Dad, and Nellie, and I just don't know how I would have done life without you."

She stopped here to clear her throat and outside, a flock of white gulls rose across a marsh like a standing ovation.

"People had donated so much to Forever Family we could afford to purchase a building, an old Victorian house on the outskirts of town, and it was such a beautiful building. All terraced and ornate, and that is when Mattie and I and your dad decided a couple of things. We decided to make it more than just a quilting outreach. We would lend out rooms in the home for veterans and families of veterans who needed a place to stay, a place away from society to collect their thoughts and heal from post-traumatic stress and to grieve the loss of loved ones.

"And God always does this, Lula, he always works when we can't. Because then we have to give him the glory."

Lula said nothing, and Clara wondered what she was thinking.

"There was one day though," Clara said, "when I kind of crashed into a hard-back chair in the kitchen, your father was moaning in the bedroom, Shane was struggling over math, you were crying because you couldn't have your friends over, and Nellie had pulled all of the encyclopedias off the bookshelf and was tearing out the pages.

"And even though Mattie was there making me a cup of tea and updating me on the veterans' home, telling me about the gardens they were putting in and how I had to go and help pick out curtains for the bedrooms, I just kind of broke across the kitchen table like one of your grandmother's teacups, the flower ones she left each of us when she died, and all of you picked up the pieces and tried to put me back together.

"That is when we decided it might be best to choose someone to oversee the whole operation, how maybe my part in it was done, and as soon as we decided it, I felt like I'd loosened my corsets or taken off my socks. You know the kind of feeling?

"I hope you do, Lula. I hope you can know how it feels to be free, you know, of everything, except happiness. To know while nothing makes sense and everything is in upheaval, you are exactly in the center of God's will. Bloody mess and all, you're there, and he's there, and when he's there, it's, well . . ."

Her breath caught. Snagged on sorrow like fabric on a sharp edge.

"Perfect. Transcending, and all the stuff the Bible talks about."

For a while it was all she could do to stare out the window and twist her fingers together and Oliver asleep, his head on her shoulder, and Shane and Lula so beautifully, gracefully, present.

Lula finally spoke. "I don't know if I've ever had such a feeling, Mama. The kind of peace you're talking about. With us having so much stuff, you wouldn't think so but most of the time I'm pretty sad. We try and do good things, you know, but it never seems enough. It feels like something's missing."

Shane smiled tenderly at his sister, pushed up his glasses on his nose, and Clara waited to see if he was going to say anything. "Reminds me a bit of the rich young man who came to Jesus in the dark," he said in his soft voice. "How he asked what he could do to get salvation, and Jesus told him to sell everything and give that money to the poor and follow him."

Lula shook her head, her pearls shimmering around her slim neck. "I don't know, Shane, selling everything just doesn't seem practical."

Clara cleared her throat. "Well, Mattie said she would do it. She would quit her job at the library and move into the Victorian house and become Director of Operations, and I said, 'Are you sure? You know you'll be surrounded by men who remind you of Gareth . . .' And she said, 'I know. But it will be my way of loving on him. Of forgiving the war, one person at a time. Of somehow staying in contact with him, through them.'

"So she did, and I thought it was the most selfless thing a person could do, to leave everything and walk into such a hard place. It reminded me a lot of Jesus. A lot of what you just said, Shane, about selling everything. Even when we have been given little, we need to be willing to leave it all, if Jesus asks us to. It doesn't mean we'll have to. For example, in our case, it meant starting a nonprofit, but for other people it might mean actually moving across the world and doing missions or something."

"That's it," said Lula, switching the stereo back on. "I can't handle much more of this, you guys. I'm feeling very judged, here."

She had Clara's temper, Clara knew this much.

"I'm so sorry, honey," said Clara. "I didn't mean to make you feel like that. I guess, you know, with my age and everything I'm just trying to share what I know, what I've learned."

Lula sighed then. "I know, Mama. I know. It's been a hard week, with everything—Daddy and Noah and it's just rough. I don't have my margarita mix here, either." She laughed, and Clara felt a sudden wash of love, one that ebbed and ached.

There was some other rock-and-roll band, now, on the radio, and Oliver was still resting on her shoulder as the fields rolled by. And Clara leaned her head on his and fell asleep.

—⟨∞⟩—

When she opened her eyes, Noah was running toward them, smiling, and the street sign behind him said Magazine Street. There was a tall stately museum-looking building, and Shane was pulling the keys from the ignition.

Oliver was still leaning on her shoulder. His head felt very heavy, and when she went to move away he didn't move. She shook him slightly with a hand that trembled, the kind of hand telling you what you're refusing to see.

"Oliver, honey, we're here," and he just drooped, and she'd always wondered how she'd respond when this happened, and here she was at seventy-seven years old and Oliver at eighty and he was too young. And she would keep getting older, now, while he stayed the same age, and she didn't scream like she always thought she would. She just made a nice bed for Oliver, tucking him amongst the blankets in the backseat, and then stepped out of the van and fell to the ground.

She didn't know she could weep words, but there they were, spilling from her eyes, because she didn't think she could express to anyone what had just happened. How do you tell people your husband has died? How do you tell your children that their father is gone?

So she held herself there on the pavement while everyone gathered around and said things. She closed her eyes tight, trying to squeeze into whatever reality Oliver was in now. Because the Bible says death is sleep, and maybe reality was thin enough to let her slip to the other side.

But they were still all there, talking to one another and trying to get her to stand up, and then she heard Noah say, "Where's Grandpa?"

Nellie let out a kind of yelp, and then Shane with, "Dad? Can you hear me? Dad?" Lula fell into hysterics, and Clara tried to shut it all out, to find her way back to Oliver, who'd left her without saying good-bye.

"He left without saying good-bye," she said, curled up there on the pavement, "he left without saying good-bye," and she found this gave her comfort, so she kept repeating the word "good-bye," even after the ambulance arrived and put her husband on a stretcher and took him away.

25

Mattie was there at the Tulane Medical Center, and they'd put Clara on a bed, too, because she'd fainted after they'd taken Oliver away.

Mattie was hushing her and holding her, and Clara was rocking and sobbing and saying, "I have to see him. Please let me see him."

It didn't surprise her to see Mattie. A good friend is someone who is always there. Period. Nothing earthly—no fight, no hurt, no words—can separate a friendship that has its footing in heaven. It's like a good marriage, Clara thought, as Mattie helped her along the hall to the nurse's station where she asked about her husband.

Clara kept saying "Sorry" to Mattie, and Mattie saying "Oh, honey, don't worry about it. It's not a big deal."

And Mattie spoke for her, there, at the nurse's station, asking to see Oliver one last time, and they told them they'd taken his body to the coroner's to be cleaned and inspected.

"That's my man you stole!" Clara said, screaming, waving her fist, her face so aflame her white hair nearly caught on fire.

"My only man, my love, and you didn't let me kiss him one more time?"

And Mattie fought in a quieter way, convincing them to let this woman say good-bye to the one person who had shared her bed, her hand, her lips, her life.

It didn't help much to see him, of course. He lay as strange as a mummy, and when Clara bent low to kiss his papery cheek, he felt cold. And he was never cold. He wore T-shirts until the first snow, and even then just a light jacket, and now he looked like winter, white all over.

She didn't know what to do after kissing him, just sort of stood there while Mattie waited in the shadows and the coroner fidgeted. The coroner looked a bit like death, too, just slightly warmed over, with vacant eyes and yellow cheeks. But she didn't care about him, only that he was going to be the one to handle her husband, but this wasn't her husband. No, this wasn't him. He was playing a joke; maybe he was hiding back upstairs, and when she got out of here he'd spring from behind a door and say, "Surprise!" in his shy way and she'd tell him it was a very bad joke. Very bad. Now let's go home and get some gelato and listen to Vivaldi and pretend we're in Venice.

They would often pretend they were in Venice. It was a place they'd always planned to go but somehow hadn't, and suddenly she had to run to the corner of the basement and vomit. Mattie took her arm and guided her back upstairs, to the long white halls of the hospital, to where her family was gathered, a crew of tears and tissue and all she wanted was her bed.

"I want to go home," she said.

They nodded and took her hands, holding her and steadying her toward the van, and then she was somehow climbing into the backseat beside the heap of blankets, Shane saying,

"No, Mom, you sit up front," and she just lay down on the blankets and went to sleep.

It was such a long ride home. Much longer than the drive there, and everyone thought so, though they did it straight without stopping to sleep, just for bathroom breaks and to let the kids run around. They ate on the road, and when the drivers got tired, they switched off.

They needed to get home to make funeral arrangements. The body would be cremated and then shipped to them, as Clara had requested, because she knew where Oliver would want to be scattered. They'd talked about this kind of thing back when death had seemed impossible.

There was war, and with it, the bitter taste of the grave, but afterward, with every new birth and every rise of a new complex building and every politician promising prosperity, death had lost its sting. Until her parents had died, and then, now. Now death stung like a hornet from hell, and Clara didn't stop feeling it the whole way home, as she lay on the blankets smelling like him. Like aftershave and earth and wood.

She wondered faintly if she could somehow seal his smell, keep it in a jar.

She knew it would come. She knew she would get angry at him because Mattie had warned her. "You will get angry at him," she'd said, after they'd emerged from the tombs of the hospital. "And when you do get angry, don't worry, don't feel guilty or bad, just let the feelings cradle you and hold you and then, just as babies grow up, let the anger grow into forgiveness and then, a new kind of love. The kind of love that resurrects the memory of your husband."

But right now it was only a deep-rooted bulb of sadness. A grieving over the way she would have cupped his face in those last moments if she'd known. Over all of the things she would have said to him, and all of the things she had said and wouldn't have.

But mostly, she was just sad because even as his head had leaned on her shoulder, his heart had slipped away and maybe, if she'd been paying more attention, she could have saved him. Just like all the others.

She'd let the one man who loved her get away. And what does one do, after that?

26

Apparently one gets out of the car and walks slowly to her apartment in Smithers (the place Clara's parents used to live in, the one she and Oliver had moved into twenty years ago after Clarence and Marie had passed away, after selling their big place in Bethlehem, because the children were grown and gone, and it was a way to keep her parents alive, Clara figured) and one makes herself a cup of tea and stands by the window not drinking it.

After a while of not drinking her tea, Clara set it down on the counter and walked into the living room where her parents' furniture remained, and she sat down in her mother's rocking chair and rocked for a long time.

Cradled her emotions the way Mattie had told her to.

Her children had offered to stay, when they dropped her off. The whole family emerging from their cars, lining up in front of the brown brick apartment building, the place her parents had bought after the diner closed down. But she wanted to be alone, she told them.

She'd said the same thing to Mattie. She'd said it with a smile and a gentle touch because she wanted Mattie to feel her forgiveness, but it was all she could do to muster the energy because Oliver was gone. He was gone, and no one could take his place.

And part of her just wanted to feel the aloneness.

She felt she owed it to him, at least.

So she sat in the chair and rocked and became accustomed to her house again, with its calm, shellfish-colored walls and its tiny lamps humming with gentle light. It was seven o'clock at night, and she and Oliver would normally be sitting down to read the paper and him to whittle at something, propping the wood in his prosthetic hand and using his right hand to chisel, and then at eight, they would turn on the old radio, the one her father used to play, and listen to it crackle out radio theater.

They would turn in at nine, creaking into bed in their old-fashioned way, and it was nothing for them to both wear flannel and socks, and yet they still slept beside each other. And this was nothing short of marvelous, Clara thought, for all of her friends who slept in separate beds, even though Oliver snored and kept her awake long past eleven. Some nights she would lie there and feel the heat from his body and count sheep.

It was something she had never regretted, this losing rest so they could sleep together. Until now, she thought, climbing into bed at night in her wool socks and her flannels and lying there alone in the dark. And she kept waiting, but Oliver never came. His side of the bed remained cold, and she'd never counted so many sheep.

After a long time of trying to keep things the same, she climbed out of bed, took her blanket and pillow, and went to sleep on the couch in the living room.

When the parcel arrived the next day, the one in bubble wrap in the shape of an urn, she didn't know how to react. Because finally her husband was home, but unwrapping him and placing him on the mantle would make it all too real. His being gone.

So for five hours she left the urn on the kitchen table and did very mundane things like snipping brown leaves from houseplants and picking up lint from the shag carpet and polishing the coffee table.

But the whole time she kept glancing toward the table where he sat. As though he were watching her from beneath those layers of bubble wrap, and finally she forced herself to sit down at three in the afternoon and carefully peel it all away, gently, as though removing old skin, and there it sat. An ivory urn with green stems chasing its sides, looping into flowers around the top, because this is what he would have wanted. To be hidden amongst his flowers.

She didn't set it on the mantle.

Rather, she took it outside into their backyard, because the apartment was on the ground floor with a patio and some lawn, and Oliver had dug gardens so you could hardly walk for all of the flowers. And they were bursting into bloom in a ferocious kind of way, all kinds of reds and oranges and purples, and she set the urn down on the bench he'd carved. She thought she might leave it there until the funeral on Friday. Because this is where Oliver always sat during the day. He would sit with some ice cold tea, the homemade kind, which they always kept in their fridge with a sprig of mint, and he would do crossword puzzles and prune his flowers and write letters to people to tell them how much God loved them.

He would do this for neighbors and politicians and friends across the country, because he was a quiet man who loved the Lord with a loud kind of love.

Once the funeral was over, she would open the urn and spread his ashes upon the dirt to let him grow there. The way he would have wanted.

The next day the cards and phone calls began to arrive. From everyone Oliver had ever talked or written to, from people who had spoken with Oliver in the barbershop, in the deli, in the post office, from customers he'd made furniture for, from ministers and elders and deacons and politicians and janitors and mechanics. And they all said one thing: "Your husband was such a loving man. Thank you for sharing him with us."

And she nodded and wept as she heard those words, as she read those words, nodded and traced the writing: scrawled in black ink, cursive in blue, clipped in pencil, and smudged with tears. Words puddled together for a man who'd sat shyly across from her in church those many years ago. For a man who'd grown friendships like he had flowers, with tenderness and care, attentive to detail, and for a man who had given her a family.

The funeral was in two days, and she didn't know what to do except sit in the backyard with the urn. And then Noah arrived, to help however she needed him to, he said, his eyebrows furrowed in an extremely grown-up way, and she held him close and he was the same height Oliver had been. And she cried.

She made him tea and cookies, and he set to work planning the ceremony, and then Mattie came, said she was moving in with Clara and wouldn't take no for an answer, because she'd gone and sold her home in Pennsylvania—the one she'd moved into after Forever Family had closed down.

And Clara just stared at her and said, "I don't know why I never saw it before."

Mattie stared back. "What?" she said.

Clara gestured with the edge of her apron. "God's love. It's in all of you. He loves me so much. So why can't I love myself?"

Mattie nodded. "Yes," she said in a whisper. "Why can't you?"

Shortly after Mattie, the others arrived, and the men helped Mattie move her belongings in: some bookcases, cardboard boxes full of books, her sewing machine, quilting supplies, and her wedding photo, along with some clothes and a wardrobe Gareth had bought her for a wedding gift.

"This is it," she said with a laugh. "I figure it's easier to not get attached to stuff if I don't have too much."

That night they all gathered, the whole family crammed into the apartment, choosing memories to share at the funeral while they sat around the fireplace with music playing through the stereo, the young kids in another room playing with old cars and balls and yo-yos.

They took turns sharing stories about Oliver. The fire snapping red and orange and the lamps a quiet gold.

"Daddy always told me I reminded him of an iris, his favorite flower," said Lula. She had brought her margarita mix and was holding one of those wide-rimmed glasses.

"He spent hours with me at the piano," said Nellie. Her long face drawn. "I was always so proud of my daddy. Of his beautiful tenor voice . . ."

Clara dabbed at her eyes with the handkerchief her mama had given her, and she thought of ripples in water. Of how a single drop falls from a canoe paddle and makes hundreds of concentric circles. It was something Oliver had pointed out to her one summer, as she wouldn't have seen them for the lake. But he was always noticing. Always caring. Always taking time.

"See how they keep on growing?" he'd said, pointing with his prosthetic on the lake that day. They'd taken the kids for a picnic down to the river outside of town, like they did most Sundays in Pennsylvania, the red-checkered blanket spread below an old oak tree, and they often brought their canoe. It was Sabbath at its finest.

"They don't let anything break them," Oliver had said. "Waves may come, but the ripples just keep expanding and multiplying. Kind of like family."

"There was the time he took me fishing," said Shane, as though he'd been in Clara's mind, and he sat beside her and she squeezed his hand. "He didn't just take me fishing though. He talked to me while we did it. We sat there and ate salted peanuts, and he laughed at my jokes and showed me the proper way to cast a line. And even the fish seemed to love him. They all just bit at the surface, and he never let us take them home. He had such a soft heart, we just threw them back in 'so they can be with their families,' he said. 'We have other meat we can eat.'"

The clock on the wall chimed one in the morning by the time the last story had been shared, the children asleep all over the room. An arm slung here, a leg there, and the adults stifling yawns and patting one another on their backs.

Then they all filed out into a night bright with stars, children over shoulders and Clara and Mattie standing at the door, watching them go. "See you tomorrow," Clara said, and then Shane turned at his car and began to sing, "Great is thy faithfulness. . . . " It had been one of Oliver's favorite hymns, and everyone joined in, there on the street corner in the dark, underneath a tapestry of light. And their voices blended into one strong tenor, rising, and for a moment she could hear Oliver again, the way his voice would reach the church rafters. Like a bird, taking flight.

27

October 2000

They were sitting in their rocking chairs—Clara in her mother's, and Mattie in hers—and they were sewing. It was Clara's favorite time of year, when the air smelled of pumpkin spice and apple cider and the trees wore brash wigs and the harvest was being rolled up like a blanket. The whole earth due for a fresh cleaning.

And she thought of how her mama never stopped cleaning, even after Daddy died of the heart attack when he was eighty-five.

He'd been flossing his teeth one night after supper on a Sunday and had just sort of keeled over and that was that. Mama said she'd never seen such a look of peace. Yet even after that summer, Mama still kept beating her rugs every fall and scrubbing her floors.

And then one September afternoon, three years later, she'd scrubbed herself to the grave. An old church friend named Marion who'd stopped by to play dominoes with Mama had found her lying there on the linoleum, between her mop and scrub brush.

So here it was, fall again, and Clara nearing the age of when her parents had died, and Oliver too. And she could smell snow in the air, she said, sitting there, sewing in the cool of the evening. Then suddenly, Clara set down her needles and started to cry.

Just shook, the whole chair vibrating, and Mattie stepped to her side. "Is it Oliver?" she said, putting a hand on Clara's shoulder. "The memories just kind of hit you, don't they?"

Clara shook her head. "No, no, it's not that. I just feel, well, useless. Like I'm sitting here, just getting old. And I miss being useful. I miss being a mom. And doing Forever Family."

It had been hard, deciding to close those doors, but it had been easy, too, one of those times when you know you've done all you can. The walls were covered in thank-you notes and photos from people with their quilts, people whose names spanned nearly a quarter century of threading fabric and patching memories. When the mayor had heard they were thinking of closing, he had offered to buy the house and turn it into a National Historic Site, and now it was. Preserved in the way good things are, keeping the memory of all those families, and she wondered why she didn't feel prouder.

Mattie was saying something, but all Clara could hear was the hum of a stir-crazy soul. She just up and went into the kitchen, pulled out a dozen bowls and clattered them to the table, tied on an apron, and began mixing bread. She dropped the five-pound bag of flour on the floor, and it slipped through her hands and made white clouds, billowing, and she should have laughed, she thought, even as she sat down and cried again.

And Mattie was there in an instant, of course she was, Clara thought, taking her friend's knotted hand and gripping it through the clouds. Flour in her hair and on her skin and when she finally stopped crying she wiped at her eyes with her apron and stood up, walked to the sink to grab a cloth, and wet it beneath a tap that gurgled and sung, and when she turned she found her footprints in the flour on the floor.

"See?" said Mattie softly. "See the way you walked there, in the mess, and left a mark? It's what you do, Clara. It's what we all do. We just keep walking. We keep walking in spite of the mess, and our feet, they make a mark. We might not see it until we turn around and look back, but it's there."

The flour settled in the way everything does, and Clara took a cloth to the table and swept up the prints and thought about it all, Mattie returning to the living room to her sewing and the quiet hum of lamplight.

And while she was wiping away the mess, she found it. Evidence of God, right there in the motion of her hands. In the presence of flour. In the firmness of the floor. She would later say it was a holy moment, but at the time, it felt very ordinary.

She didn't need to save anyone. She couldn't. She couldn't even bake bread. And it was okay. Because God still loved her. He had given her hands with which to create and a floor to walk on and flour to bake with, and she could try, try again, but she didn't have to. She didn't need to bake bread. She just needed to try. To use these hands he'd given her, and this flour, and to create in the image she'd been made in.

She sat there, day dawning even as it ended, the light of something pure spreading across her seventy-seven-year-old skin. She pulled off her apron and hung it serenely on the nail in the wall and then grabbed her hat and pinned it onto her white hair, the hat with the bright blue feather she'd bought so many years ago, and then she stepped out into air that seemed brighter, somehow, like angels had descended. And she wondered if she were going crazy, but didn't mind much if she was.

It was a freedom she'd felt just a few times in her life. She remembered vaguely crayons and paper and a delirious scribbling of color on white, and there was the time she'd gone skinny-dipping in the river with Eva, and then graduating nursing school, skipping down the street and Eva's yellow hair like birds' wings flying.

She scrunched her eyes as she stepped on broken leaves, and the air smelled of fermented apples. Around her everything was dying, but it was very natural, she realized, this dying. It brought the newness the earth was aching for. Death led to life and to resurrection, and even though she had sprinkled Oliver's ashes on his flower beds, he wasn't there. And Gareth wasn't buried in France alongside piles of other soldiers. Her daddy and mama weren't buried in Smithers' church cemetery. They were all alive and singing and would never die again. And it wasn't her fault. She had done her part. She had made their life more bearable, more loving, while they were alive, and it wasn't her job to save. She couldn't even save herself.

It was so dark by now she could barely see her hands, and she realized she could barely see the road, out here in the country past the town limits, and she suddenly wondered at herself and laughed a little, because she was losing her way a lot these days. Then she stopped laughing because she realized this time, she had no family nearby to rescue her and Mattie didn't drive or have a car and was probably fast asleep in her chair.

She kept walking as though praying with her feet and scouring the horizon for some kind of light. The stars suddenly seemed very far away and the moon had disappeared behind a cloud. Then, a patch of light, a square box of solid flame shining into the darkness across the field, and as she approached, on swollen ankles, her heart beating inside her head and her eyes watery, she found a window, with no curtains, just a single wildflower dried up in a vase on the sill.

As she approached the door whose paint was peeling it was ajar, and she could hear a child sobbing and the sound of little feet and the squeak of a chair on the floor.

As she knocked at the door, it opened to reveal a dirty kitchen with seven children around a table and no mother or father, all a range of faces, and one of them was crying and clutching her stomach.

The girl at the end of the table seemed older than the rest, but barely, all skin and bones stretched into freckles and red hair, and she was dishing out what seemed like watery soup. "It was all I could find," she said in a quiet voice. "But Daddy will come home soon . . ."

"And then what?" said a boy with a pointed face, his fists curled and his shirt hanging off him.

Clara cleared her throat, and they turned, and the girl with the freckles stood. "What do you want?" she said.

Seven pairs of eyes and Clara held onto the door frame. "I'm sorry, I seem to have lost my way. Would you mind if I used your phone?"

"We ain't got one," said the little girl who had been crying, her eyes like streaked windows.

"Oh, sorry to bother you," said Clara, and she turned to go.

"Want some soup?" the same girl said.

They didn't have much and she wasn't hungry, but she sat among them, anyway, with this crew of children in their faded shirts and shorts, and none of them wore shoes. The tap dripped the whole time into a rusty sink. There was a draft through the walls, and the soup was mostly water with some chopped-up potatoes and carrots. They licked their bowls when they were done, then sucked on their fingers. She divided her bowlful among them. Wan smiles, and then it was gone.

Heavy footsteps outside the door and the girl with the freckles, whose name was Sarah, swept the bowls off the table, and the kids ran in different directions, and Clara just kind of sat there wondering what had happened.

The footsteps stopped, and there was the thump of what seemed boots, and then the door creaked open. And he stood there. A skinny, short man like a crooked branch, with the angriest eyes Clara had ever seen, and he stepped across the threshold and slammed the broken door and said, "Get off my property!"

Sarah stepped up, her hands twisting. "Daddy, this ain't Social Services. This here is Mrs. Clara from up the road. She got lost goin' for a walk and was just biding her time till she got her bearings."

Clara stood, knocking over her chair and rubbing her hands on her skirt, and the man spit as he stepped past her and said, "I'm hungry." Sarah scooped the remaining soup into a bowl, and he took one look at it and threw it at the sink and yelled, "What am I, a dog? It's your fault we're all going hungry, girl. If your mother were alive she'd be schooling you. She was the finest cook, that woman," and he stepped down the hall and slammed a door. Sarah didn't even cry, just let out a breath and nodded at Clara.

"You best be goin'. He's had plenty to drink today."

Clara nodded.

"I can see that," she said. "Will he hurt you?"

Sarah shook her head. "No, he's all bark, no bite. Mama passed away a year ago. We didn't have insurance to cover her hospital bills. Anyway, he was never nice. My mama was a sucker for the wrong kind of men, and he was the one she found after our Daddy died . . ."

She blushed to her scalp and stammered. "But you don't want to hear all of this."

Clara put a hand in her cardigan pocket, feeling for paper, but there was none. "Give me your palm and a pen," and the girl did, and she scribbled down her address. "For when you need it," Clara said.

Then Sarah nodded and walked her to the porch, pointed her toward town, and Clara stepped out in her tan leather shoes, the moon emerging from the clouds, a golden globe in the sky.

And even as she walked the long path home in the dark, she thought about light. How hopeful the square patch of window in the night. How it had led her to God's next plan.

Eva had been that light growing up. Gareth had been that light in the war. Mattie had been the light of friendship, and Oliver, the light of love. The light of a thousand years.

And it never gets so dark that you can't find it, Clara figured.

The light that will lead you home.

Discussion Questions

1. Who is Clara's namesake, and how is she influential in Clara's vocation? How are the qualities of Clara's namesake reflected in the main protagonist as she ages? (Chapter 1)

2. Clara's friendship with Eva is one that saved her as a child. Why is this? How does this relationship evolve, and why does it eventually end? (Chapters 2–4)

3. Why does Clara refuse Timmy's gift of the Psalms? How has she been jaded by religion, and what role does her father, the Reverend Clarence Wilson, play in this? (Chapter 4)

4. What event in France causes Clara to stop sleeping? When she does manage to sleep, what does she dream about? (Chapter 5)

5. How does meeting Gareth reconcile faith and justice for Clara as well as give her a mission upon returning to America? (Chapters 5 and 8)

6. Why is Clara both pleased and saddened by what she finds at home? How have her mama and papa changed? What is at the root of Marie's silence? (Chapters 9 and 11)

7. What is it about Mattie's quilt that brings hope not only to new mothers but also to Marie? (Chapter 11)

8. Talk about the qualities that Oliver possesses and what attracts Clara to him. How does he quietly pursue her, and why does she decide to put a stop to his efforts? (Chapters 9 and 12)

9. What happens to make Clara admit her love for Oliver, and how does she witness the pieces of a promise coming together, like a quilt? (Chapters 15 and 16)

10. How does Clara's lifestyle change in Pennsylvania? What inspires her to start a nonprofit organization with Mattie? (Chapters 17–19, 21)

11. Eighty-year-old Oliver is determined to drive the entire trip to New Orleans. Why? And why does Clara regret letting him? (Chapter 20)

12. How does the retelling of Clara's life story affect her eldest grandson, Noah, and motivate him to steal the quilt? (Chapter 23)

13. What is Clara's greatest fear, and how does she face this fear when they arrive in New Orleans? (Chapters 24 and 25)

14. What event threatens to end Clara's friendship with Mattie? How does Mattie's faithfulness to Clara reflect God's love for us? (Chapters 22, 25, and 26)

15. In the final chapter, what is the light that leads Clara home, and how does it suggest purpose for Clara's future? (Chapter 27)

Want to learn more about author
Emily T. Wierenga and check out other great
fiction from Abingdon Press?

Sign up for our fiction newsletter at
www.AbingdonPress.com
to read interviews with your favorite authors, find tips
for starting a reading group, and stay posted on what
new titles are on the horizon. It's a place to connect
with other fiction readers or post a
comment about this book.

Be sure to visit Emily online!

www.emilywierenga.com

We hope you enjoyed *A Promise in Pieces* and that you will continue to read the Quilts of Love series of books from Abingdon Press. Here's an excerpt from *A Stitch and a Prayer.*

1

January 1899
Near the Willamette River
Wilsonville, Oregon

Whenever the wind blew hard and the rain came down sideways lashing the windowpane, Florence Harms heard her dancing song. As the wind increased, so did the song. It sang of distant mountain peaks and torturous trails winding through giant boulders. It sang of sweat and blood and always it climbed upwards, trembling from the heights, beckoning, calling, its strange haunting melody set her feet to dancing.

A part of her wanted to whirl, stamp, and lift her arms to embrace the music, to move in unison to the raging wind and the flutter of the flame within the lantern bathing the cabin's empty room in its soft glow. But the other part was fearful, her hand still clinging to the cane as her body slowly became more mobile, putting aside forever, or so she hoped, the illness that took her ability to walk and run freely, her energy to do her daily tasks.

The good doctor told her she had taken a turn for the better and she could expect to return to her full energy and freedom of movement. But it would take time. Will had returned from the icy north and soon, even before winter ended, she would become his wife.

"Except I always wanted roses on my wedding day," she whispered into the silent room of the newly constructed log cabin Will and the men from Frog Pond Church had banded together to raise.

The day after Christmas they felled the young firs in the grove along the back field, cut them into lengths the horses dragged to the site she and Will had chosen at the edge of the garden. It had only taken another few days to raise the walls and put up the roof, using shakes cut from an old-growth fir tree felled several years earlier. All they needed now was the order of glass windows to arrive by steamboat.

But would it arrive? Whenever it rained steadily, she remembered 1894, the year of the flood. Since then, from her home on the West Hills of Portland, she had always kept a close watch on the river whenever the rains refused to let up. Would there be flooding along the waterfront come morning? And what about the boats and barges? Would they be swept out to the mighty Columbia River and on into the ocean?

Florence pushed her thoughts away from the year when First Street had flooded and tried to recapture her song. She was in a safe place now, high above the creek that raced through the canyon during high water. No longer would she live in a tent, she'd be safe with Will in the cabin he was building for her.

Instead, there was a loud knock. She whirled around to face the door. Who would be out on a rain-drenched afternoon fast turning into darkness? Tilly? Her Aunt Amelia?

The front door blew open as she leaned forward on her cane and rose to her feet. "Will!" She gasped then smiled at the tall, broad-shouldered man with the worried frown. He stood on the threshold, water dripping off the brim of his hat and streaking his coat. She held out both hands and he ran to her while her heart danced and twirled and spun inside her.

"Oh, Will," she whispered. She longed to reach up and caress his cheek with her fingertips, but he held her hands tight. She caught her breath, his tender smile put lights into his blue eyes, and the rough hands tightening over hers trembled. Will, how dear you are.

As the coldness of his hands penetrated hers, she stepped back. "Goodness, you're freezing to death!" She looked down. Mud spattered his trousers and his boots attested to the heavy rain and thick garden mud stirred up by the horse's hooves and the men's boots.

"I can't believe you did this. Nobody knew where you were, not Tilly and not your aunt." His voice softened. "Besides, I—I wanted to be the first to show you our new home."

"I'm sorry," she said. "I just didn't think." Heat rose into her face. "I guess deep inside I'm still the little girl who wants to know what's wrapped inside the pretty packages. I just couldn't wait."

A sudden chill ran down her arms and she pressed closer into his arms, felt them tighten around her. "I can't believe you're really here. It's like I'm asleep and dreaming and I'm afraid to wake up."

"And if you are, I promise, I won't be gone."

"But what if—if you're not there?"

"But I will be there. And if I have to leave—for any reason—I'll let you know."

He bent his head and kissed her tenderly, deeply without holding back. "We're going to be married," he murmured as he trailed his fingertips along her cheekbone. "I know what it's like to want, and have to wait."

"But what if I can't be the wife you need?" she whispered. "I'm tired of weariness and wanting to cry, sometimes without any real reason."

"But Dr. Rutler says not to worry." He gently released her and guided her toward the workbench someone had shoved beneath the window ledge.

"But I do worry," she protested, as she sank onto the bench. "Not so much for me, but for you. Are you sure we shouldn't wait until spring returns? Perhaps by then the warmer weather will ease the pain and swelling in my joints."

Will shook his head. "I waited too long already. It's like I told you back then, in sickness or in health, I want you to be my wife. I still do, now perhaps more than ever. You are beautiful to me, just the way you are."

He took her hands in his and raised them to his lips. Gently, like the touch of butterfly wings, he kissed her swollen knuckles and then her wrist. "I love you, Florence. You are God's gift to me."

Afterward, he knelt beside her, resting his elbows on the window ledge, his chin cupped in his hands. "Have you been to the spring lately? It's one of the places I love most here, the cedars overshadowing it with their branches, the water dripping over mossy rocks into the deep pool surrounded by maidenhair fern."

His blue eyes darkened as he looked toward a place she had not seen in a long time. "I saw deer and coon tracks, even squirrels, and other wild creatures go there to drink. It's the perfect place. The creek below, and overhead more trees, giant maples and firs so tall they look like they're trying to touch the sky.

Florence smiled. "Don't forget the dipper tied to the branch. It's the first thing I saw when I pushed back the vine maple branches at the end of the path. It was like entering a safe place waiting just for me and gave me the feeling of coming home. And I was, but I didn't know it then." She sighed. "I wish I could go back there, but 'it's not possible. At least not now."

"But I could go with you, even carry you if you needed me to."

"But the rain," she protested. "Why the mud on the paths would send us end over teakettle. Let's leave the water fetching to the young ones for a while. We'll take our turns later."

"I'm glad Tilly's here, especially this winter. She's a great girl, so is Hal's nephew; the redhead who's sweet on her. They make a cute couple."

"Yes, they do. I wouldn't be too surprised if they wed this summer. But we'd better get back to the tent. No sense worrying the family."

She paused as a worried frown creased his forehead. "It's who we are now, Will. Aunt Amelia, you and me, Tilly and her little sister. For better or worse, it's the way it is. We're a family."

"But, it doesn't mean . . ."

"No, it doesn't mean they'll be staying with us after we're married. Besides, Aunt Amelia has her own resources. And, yes, the girls do have their little place on the other side of the settlement. But they're all alone. Their father, even their aunt, and the boyfriend she ran off with are still in the Klondike, at least as far as they know. They've had no word. Right now, they need us—and we need them. "

"But where will they . . ."

"Where will they sleep? They'll be in the tent. We'll be in the cabin." Her gaze wandered out the window. She could see the dark brown soil of the garden, the firs beyond, the road curving out of sight into the canyon below where birds sang in the spring and wild creatures lived and roamed.

"This window with the bench is my best spot," Florence confided. "I hope we sit here often, together, looking out the window, watching for spring, perhaps even put up a fence to keep the deer out of the yard. We can plant hollyhocks and Heartsease when the soil warms."

Will got to his feet and again took her into his arms. "And your mother's rose." He gestured toward the open window. "Tomorrow, I'll dig it up from beside the tent and plant it where we can see it from here. Of all the gifts we'll receive on our wedding day, the gift we'll treasure most will be your mother's rose."

"That and Mother's pearls." She laughed. "Just think I'll be able to wear them on my wedding day!"

Will smiled. "You haven't taken them off since I've arrived home from the Klondike at Christmastime, have you?"

"No," she whispered, as she slowly and awkwardly struggled with the top button of her coat.

"Here, I'll help you!" Will exclaimed. His hand came over hers, and he undid the button beneath her chin. Florence's hand slid beneath the collar, then around her throat.

"Will," she gasped, her voice hoarse with fear. Her stomach dipped downwards. "The pearls, I'm not wearing mother's heirloom pearls. They're gone. I had them on this morning, I know I did. I saw them in the mirror when I put up my hair."

For a moment, her hands covered her face. "I can't believe I lost them," she wailed. "Almost more than anything I want to wear them on my wedding day. And now, look what I've done! They could be anywhere, here, on the path, even in the tent."

Will reassured her. "We'll find them, Florence. They can't be far, they can't be. We'll look everywhere, spread the word. Aunt Amelia, Tilly, Faye; one of us is bound to find them."

He took her arm and they walked slowly through the front room and into the smaller back room, pushing aside building debris and sawdust that lay cross the board floor. It felt like it took forever. He reached for her hand, then with the lantern in the other, he guided her out the door, the faint fluttering flame their only light to push back the shadows.

There was no pearl necklace shining through the brown leaves moldering on the path, no tangled necklace caught in the underbrush grabbing at their clothing.

Tilly met them at the doorway leading into the tent. She took one look at Florence's face. "Are you all right?" She turned toward Will, noted the consternation written by the twisting movement of his lips, the worry in his blue eyes. "What happened?" she asked. "Where have you been?"

"Just over to the cabin," Florence explained. "I—I shouldn't have gone alone, but I did. Will found me there. And then I discovered the pearl necklace wasn't around my neck. She reached for her handkerchief and wiped away tears threatening to run down her cheeks. "We looked everywhere, the cabin, the trail, even held the lantern high to see if a stray branch might have grasped it up as it fell off my neck. But we saw nothing, it was getting too dark."

Aunt Amelia came up behind Florence and put her arm around her. "Did you have it this morning when you wakened? It might very well be here in the tent. If you want me to, I can help you look through your things."

"And if it isn't here we can check the path again when daylight comes," Florence replied. "Oh, Aunt Amelia, I'm so sorry. You kept mother's pearls when she gave them to you for safe keeping before the train wreck that claimed her life. I—I only had the necklace a little while and already I've lost it twice, once on the river when the steamboat we were on collided with another. I'll never forget when how awful I felt when the trunk with the pearls was swept overboard, and disappeared beneath the water." Her lips trembled, "Now I've lost them again."

"Now, now, dear. No more tears. What is lost doesn't necessarily stay lost. And you know praying makes a big lot of difference, girl. Like you said, them pearls have been lost before and not so long ago either."

⊸∞⊸

As the rains increased and the waters of the river rose, the steamboats stopped plying up and down the Willamette. Will, anxious to find work after his return from the gold rush, found a temporary job in the feed store on Main Street, close to Hal's Mercantile. He even found a nearby boarding house, which was, as he put it, "'a shade above sharing the horse and goat's accommodations.'"

The school remained open and Tilly spent most days accompanying Faye on horseback, thereby increasing Aunt Amelia and Florence's workload. And Tilly continued to bring a supply of water and wood into the tent to meet each day's need before she and Faye left. Nor did she forget to search for the missing necklace. She even donned Florence's cape and went out several times into the rain at daylight to search the path; then she searched the newly raised log cabin.

Although the couple had originally planned to have a simple ceremony in the tent, their plans changed when Mrs. Moad offered them the use of their home less than a mile away. "John is willing to fetch the four of you in our covered wagon—the same wagon John's-great grandmother came in to Oregon, actually to the same property where our house was built. His father finished the bedroom downstairs—there you can dress. It will be perfect. I can play the organ in our front room while the Reverend comes in, then Will of course, then you in your white dress. What do you think?"

"I think it would be wonderful," Florence whispered. "But I still don't know when we'll be ready."

"Once these rains stop and the boats start running, you're going to be a beautiful couple," she said, and she was right. On the first Saturday in February, instead of the first Saturday in January as they had originally planned, the family was ready to depart for their neighbor's home.

A watery sun peeked out through the clouds and streamed over the tent as John drove his team into the clearing in front of the cabin. First Aunt Amelia, Florence using her cane, and Tilly came down the path.

"Now where did the child disappear to?" Aunt Amelia fretted. "She was here a minute ago and now she's gone." She snapped her fingers. "Gone, just like that."

"She's coming," John said, "don't you worry none, she's on her way."

Even as he spoke, Faye exploded from the bushes at the clearing's edge, running as fast as she could toward them. "I found them! I found them!" she screamed. "Blue had them all the time."

"Why, Child," Aunt Amelia exclaimed as she held out her hand. But it was into Florence's open palm Faye laid the missing pearl necklace.

"I knew they'd come home," the child cried. "But why did the cat take them? I prayed and prayed. But why did God wait so long? I'd really like to know."

Tears blurred Florence's eyes as she held the creamy luster of the pearls against her pale wrist. The touch of the jewels brought her thoughts backward into the past. She reached down and pulled Faye close. "Oh, Honey," she exclaimed. "I don't know why or all the answers, but I know some of them."

She looked up and her dark brown eyes met John's gaze. "When Will first asked me to be his wife, I said 'no,' I loved him but couldn't marry him unless we had a house with a wide porch and white pillars. In my mind, I saw a house much like yours and Martha's, John." Her hand reached up and covered her mouth to hide the sudden quiver of her lips.

She took a deep breath and continued. "All my life my parents and us kids lived in one shack after another. When they were both killed in a train accident, I went to live with my older brother, Richard, and his wife, Opal, in Portland's West Hills. Even while I grieved the loss of my parents, the beauty around me, the gardens, my bedroom, even their parlor so filled with lovely things nourished my spirit."

For a moment, she covered her face with her hands even as Aunt Amelia put her arms around her. "Florence, it's over now. Let it go."

Florence lifted her tear stained face to her family. "It's just what I am doing. You see, I loved Will, but I was afraid when he told me I'd have to live in a tent until he could build us a log cabin on the farm he'd just bought. I—I sent him away. I know now I would have regretted it forever, if Aunt Amelia hadn't urged me to follow my heart and go after him."

Her gaze clung to Aunt Amelia's and they both smiled. "You came with me when I followed Will to this clearing in the woods. But he was gone; he loved me so much he followed the gold rush into the icy north so he could strike it rich and build me the house of my dreams."

She turned and looked back at the tent she was leaving. "I haven't yet learned all I have to learn here, but one thing I do know; people are more important than things. There's even a verse in my Bible I'm learning from. I found it at Christmas time when Tilly and I opened the leather chest holding mother's pearls. There in the bottom of the leather chest was a secret drawer and inside were little notes she'd written.

"When we didn't find the pearl necklace I took out one of the notes and read a verse where she'd written the notation: 'my life verse.' I took the verse for my own, even memorized it when I was worrying over the pearl necklace, the windows for the cabin which didn't arrive, and our wedding having to be postponed."

Aunt Amelia could keep silent no longer, "Well for pity's sake, Child," she exclaimed, "what was it?"

John interrupted. "We need to get going."

"You mean Mother's life verse?" Florence asked.

"Yes," everyone chorused.

Florence lifted her chin, her voice came through clear and strong. "From Colossians, chapter three, verses one and two. 'If ye then be risen with Christ, seek those things which are above, where Christ sitteth on the right hand of God. Set your affection on things above, not on things on the earth.'"

"'It's what I want my marriage to be." She turned and looked at each person standing with her. "You are my witnesses," she said. "You have my permission to tell me if I'm not living according to those precepts."

Faye grabbed Florence's hand. She smiled. "I think I understand a little bit better now."

When Aunt Amelia, Faye, and Tilly climbed into the back of the wagon, John carefully helped Florence into the front seat. His "we're off," echoed across the fields.

The horses lunged, the wagon lurched. Aunt Amelia, sitting on the bench John had nailed into place on the wagon floor for their comfort, leaned forward and gently touched the hood of the cape covering Florence's shining dark hair.

"May God bless you and the good man God has chosen to be your husband," she said softly. "And you will be blessed."